The Bandana boy

To Brandon,

I hope that this story of a hero inspires you to be the hero of your own story. Thank you for supporting this dream of mine, and I appreciate the friendship that we are forming. It is an honor to be signing this page for you and I truly hope that you enjoy your escape...

Love, Ryan [illegible]

To Brandon,

I hope that this story of a hero inspires you to be the hero of your own story. Thank you for supporting this dream of mine, and I appreciate the friendship that we are forming. It is an honor to be signing this page for you and I truly hope that you enjoy your escape...

Love, [illegible]

The Bandana boy

Ryan Anthony Dube

ISBN-13: 978-0-578-57720-3

Dedication

I promised my mother that I would never stop writing and I never will. This is for those whom I could not save.

Is it a sin to kill a mockingbird?
What if it has two broken wings and can't sing?
With no song and without flight what is left for a bird's life?
What a shame it is to have to kill a mockingbird.

Prologue: The Boy with the Bandana

The small boy sat cross-legged on his bedroom floor, eyes swirling, staring blankly at the crack in the frosted window. Visions of fantasy flickered across his subconscious, his attention entranced in epics of heroism, his existence so deeply rooted in the world that he had created for himself that he did not hear the real world crashing down around him. The door to his bedroom flung violently open as his mother rushed in with blood covering her battered face, sobbing in a demoralized rage. The boy blinked himself back to reality as he silently watched his mom scavenge through the shallow closet, throwing worn clothes and old shoes into a tattered suitcase. Her furious energy spun her in circles. Her wild eyes scanned the room frantically before coming to a dead stop on the kaleidoscopic irises of her five-year-old son.

Her steady stare was cold and unfamiliar. She held her gaze with an unnatural absence until the slow dripping of blood from a cut on her forehead finally forced her to blink. Her left eye was beginning to swell shut, her lips were badly split and her nose was twisted and leaking. She reached up slowly and ran a gentle finger across the gashes in her skin, pushing aside the loose hairs that were dangling in her cuts. She leaned against the wall and opened her mouth as if there were something to be said, but she wordlessly sank to the ground, defeated and humiliated, with rebellious tears streaking down her punished cheeks.

The small boy rose to his feet and took a cautious step towards his sunken mother who was cowering into herself. She waved away her son with one weak hand as the other tried to clot the blood and tears as they escaped her. The boy placed a nervous palm on her swollen cheek and after a moment of resistance the weight of her head fell softly into his tiny hand. A fragile smile snuck across her lips as her son hugged her neck and curled up into her lap.

She held him with all of the strength that he gave her. She held him the way that he held her life together. She pressed a kiss into the top of his messy head. Her fingertips hovered over the scattered bruises that marked the boy's neck, back and arms and she shook her head with finality.

"No more," she whispered into the boy's ear.

She rocked her son and lifted him onto the edge of his bed and then grabbed an empty backpack to finish packing his things. She threw in everything that was within reach – a plastic baseball glove, a bundle of cartoon underwear, and a pair of coverless picture books that were missing pages. She stuffed in a stiff square blanket from under the bed and tossed in a pair of metal cars that had crashed on the carpet. The boy tapped his mother's shoulder and held out an action figure that had been posing bravely on the nightstand. She took one look at the overflowing backpack and shook her head, but before the inevitable guilt could rush in she forced the toy into a side pocket and began to fight with the busted zipper.

As she struggled to close the bag, an annoyed sigh came from the doorway behind her where a broad, tired man dauntingly filled the frame, rubbing his chin with scraped knuckles.

"Can't we just talk about this?" The man's lazy voice crawled across the room as the young mother stepped in front of her son. He laughed and threw up his hands in innocent protest before fidgeting with his belt buckle.

"I don't want to do this in front of your child," he mumbled with a routine numbness.

The boy's mother threw down her son's backpack in disgust and took wild, uncalculated strides towards the man until they were face to face.

"If you ever put your hands on me again," she said, lifting a finger to his chest, "I will kill you."

The man swatted at her hand and gave a condescending chuckle but she didn't waiver.

"You know that you can't live without me," he slurred, taking a clumsy step towards her as she quickly shifted her feet.

"Then I will kill us both."

The deadly promise froze the room and the small boy stole a nervous glance at his mother.

The man seemed genuinely confused by her defiance. "Do you think that I'm scared of you?"

She began to shake her head hysterically, her voice scraping out in barely a whisper, "You don't have to be…you don't have to be scared…you don't have to be."

She reached back and grabbed her son's hand without taking her manic eyes off of the monster in front of her. "We would like to leave now. Please."

There was a moment of silence in which there was no air left in the room to breathe.

"Then leave."

The man turned himself sideways in the doorway and created a small space just wide enough for them to squeeze through. She dragged her son behind her and muttered an empty thank you as she brushed past. The hallway that led to their escape seemed to stretch on forever. She felt like she was trying to run in a dream, but this was a nightmare. She realized that it was all a cruel metaphor – a sickening and infinite reminder of the cycle of perpetual pain and false hope that she had allowed herself to grow accustomed to. She knew there was no escape, only an end to it altogether, one way or the other. Thus, when she lunged for the handle of the back door, there wasn't even the slightest part of her that believed it would be open.

She shook the knob, pounded on the screen and pleaded with gods whose ears never seemed to hear her part of the world. The stalking man came up from behind, took her by the hair, and kicked the boy to the ground. She flailed her arms and dug her nails into his eyes and nose. As she struggled, the man continued to yank at her hair, wrenching her neck until it seemed on the verge of snapping. The moment she gave up the fight she was flung recklessly, headfirst into the wall. Her body went limp and she crumpled messily into a pile next to the door. The small boy crawled between the man's legs and laid on top of his mother. He wrapped his arms around her and braced himself.

The towering man looked down on them clinging together pathetically. The man hinged over at the waist and stooped to place a sword-like finger under the little boy's chin. He held his threat against the boy's throat until the dramatics of fear no longer entertained him and he walked away indifferently. The man grabbed his keys from the kitchen and gave them a high toss into the air, but he fumbled the catch and they crashed to the floor. He picked up the fallen keys and threw them up again, this time successfully snagging them out of the air. He then walked coolly out of the front door as if he never dropped them.

***

There was a pretty girl in a yellow dress standing next to a red tree in an empty park with her arms crossed in front of her chest. The steady wind blew her long blonde hair sideways across her face, so that only her toothy smile could be seen. The small boy stood across from her with his arms behind his back, his feet together, and his shirt tucked in. The pretty girl with the long hair and the yellow dress counted down from three and the small boy with his shirt tucked in began to chase her around the red tree. They spun in careless circles, turning and twisting with the breeze like falling leaves. The boy chased the girl with his arms outstretched through the green grass and the purple flowers, with a laugh on his lips and the golden sun warming his bare feet.

As the laughing boy caught up to the giggling girl she disappeared through the air and popped up on the other side of the tree. She began to taunt the boy with a wiggle of her nose and a flick of her hair. She stuck her tongue out and put her thumbs in her ears as the playful boy gave chase once more. As she ran from the boy with her arms by her sides, she dragged her nails through the air and peeled a rainbow out of the bright blue backdrop of the sky. The flowing colors trailed behind her every buoyant step like a comet's tail, as she and the boy revolved weightlessly around the tree in the empty park.

The girl at the end of the rainbow stopped to pick a flower that was growing in a patch. She put her lips on the stem and blew up the flower like a balloon until it was as tall as the giant tree. The girl planted the flower back into the ground and began to climb it. A small singing bird landed on the shoulder of the boy as he watched the girl in the yellow dress swing herself onto the highest branch of the giant tree. She pulled her knees into her chest and rocked herself to the melodic sounds of the bird's song.

As the boy smiled and the girl swayed, a dark gray cloud rolled above and cast a shadow over their perfect park. Thunder rumbled, rain ran down, and lightning flashed and struck the tree. Within a moment, all was gone except for the piercing song of the mockingbird, crying out for help.

***

The small boy sat up straight at the end of his bed with his blanket pulled up to his chin, shivering from both fear and the frosted air that seeped through the crack in the glass. In the world outside of the window, snow fell in teasingly peaceful flurries, performing graceful, acrobatic routines beneath the warm glow of the street lamps. The powder fell evenly across the bus benches and decorated the branches of the barren trees.

But the boy didn't live in that world.

The chilled child watched the clouds from his breath create their own storm in front of his nose and while his bones trembled, his thoughts wandered back to his imaginary park. His mind had betrayed him. He had been trapped inside of his escape. Reality had found him in his safest place. It soon became clear to the boy, as his swirling eyes came to a stop on his shuddering mother, curled into a ball with her knees tucked to her chest, that tonight he wouldn't be safe anywhere.

His mother held her chin in her hand with her elbow on her knee, absently pushing hair behind her ears and adjusting the bandana she had wrapped around the gash on the top of her head. With a heavy heart, she looked up and held her son's fragile gaze, examining the mysteriously shifting colors of his eyes. She blew him a kiss from her cracked lips. She truly adored her precious son and he loved his gorgeous mother.

There was no deception in the truth of her beauty. She had a slim face with edges like a crescent moon, curly blonde hair that spiraled like golden staircases, extraordinary hazel eyes that pulled in like the tide and a smile that rose slowly like a summer wave. The fates had forced her to grow up quickly, but still she radiated with an undeniable exuberance that played true to her youth. After all, she was still just a baby herself when she was given one of her own.

So as she sat on the stained carpet, deflated and embarrassed, she tried to exhale her pain and breathe in her reality. All of her life she had been a magnet for affection and a model of society. She was everything she knew that the world wanted her to be. There was no doubt that her future would be as impressive as promised, but as she would soon find out, the universe could be disturbingly random. It was just another night of being underage and under the influence, an innocent enough distraction from being constantly swallowed by her own perfection. Had it been just another night there would be no story to tell, but the problem was that she didn't remember anything from the evening out, except of course that she lost her favorite necklace and that four weeks later her pregnancy test was positive. She panicked and tried to shelter her secret but the city had too many eyes. She lost everyone close to her who had only loved the idea of who she was and who they thought she would become. With nowhere to hide she chose to run, dropping out of school, leaving everyone and everything behind. So she knew how, but could never comprehend why she was bloodied and battered, staring at her child through swollen eyes, a boy who had diverted her destiny by becoming it.

"Did you have a bad dream?"

The boy nodded.

"So did I," she joked, pointing at her bruises and laughing harmlessly at herself.

She gingerly worked her back up the wall until she was on her feet and slid herself onto the corner of the bed facing her boy. She watched him thoughtfully before leaning forward and scrunching her nose.

"What's going on in that mind of yours? What kind of crazy life are you living in there? Huh?" she whispered to him lightly. The boy shrugged and bashfully pulled the blanket up to his face once more.

"Aw, my shy boy," she teased, pinching his cheek.

The boy shook his head and pouted.

"I know, I know..." She ran her fingers through his hair. "You aren't shy, you just like to listen."

She paused.

"Actually, there is something that I need you to hear." She glanced over her shoulder towards the door. The boy followed his mom's gaze and saw a silver kitchen knife lying on the ground.

"I need you to listen to me love; I need you to really listen. Okay?"

The boy nodded and she cleared her throat.

"I just want to say – no – I have to say that I don't know how much longer I have left to be a mother to you...and I know that I could have done better at being your mother, and I hate myself every day for it, but hating myself doesn't make me better at taking care of you. I just want to protect you from everything that is out there...even though it's obvious that I am not much help to you."

The boy's mother choked up.

"I'm sorry. For everything. For the fact that *this* is the best life that I could give you. You aren't supposed to go through the rest of this all on your own. I am supposed to be there because I am your mother."

She pounded her fist into her leg.

"I am supposed to help you with your homework until you get so smart that you have to help me with it. I am supposed to hold your hand while you cross the street until I am so old that you have to hold my hand to get me across. That's all I want. Am I asking for too much?"

She placed her open palm on her chest.

"Look, I don't know what it's like to be a good mom. I really don't baby, but I know that I could have been one because I love you so much – much more than you will ever know… and maybe one day you won't believe me."

She turned her head away, covering her mouth with both hands trying to silence her heavy sobs. She took a long, uneasy breath before continuing.

"I have made so many mistakes in my life that I'll never remember the first or last one…but having you is the greatest thing I have ever done or will ever do and I am proud of that."

She wiped at her eyes.

"There is so much pain in this world; it can all be so scary and lonely. I wish that I could shelter you from it all but I can't. I just can't. But please don't be afraid, and don't ever wonder if someone out there loves you because the answer will always be yes. The answer will always be me. Ok?"

The boy nodded his head sincerely, not understanding what his mother was telling him, but understanding that she needed him to hear it.

"And one last thing," she added.

"If you love someone, if you really love them, ask them what their favorite color is. As soon as you know what color is their favorite it feels like you have known them forever. It's the best piece of advice I've ever gotten, and maybe the only one I actually remembered. So, there you go."

The young mother tossed her hands up and forced a smile. She gave her son a tender kiss on the forehead and then nudged him with her nose. She made a chomping sound with her mouth and pretended to bite his neck.

"You are so cute I could eat you alive. It would only take one bite!"

She dug her fingers into his sides and he squirmed to escape her ticklish grip. While trying to break free, a flailing elbow landed squarely on the bridge of his mother's already fractured nose. She grimaced and held her face as the boy backed away and tucked his hands under his armpits. A thick drop of blood rolled down to the end of her finger and she flicked it away tiredly.

"I think it's time for bed, baby," she said, scooping him up and laying his head gently on the pillow. She tucked in the sheet tightly at all of the corners and by the time the layers were snug the boy had already crawled out from beneath the covers. He sat up straight with his hands folded in front of him. His mother put her hands on her hips, but the boy sustained his silent plea. She rolled her eyes and reached down into the broken backpack on the floor and pulled out the picture books that were missing their covers. She held one up in each hand.

"What are you thinking, bub? Two classics, our two favorites, we already know how each one goes, we read them every night. Which is it going to be?"

The boy's eyes bounced back and forth as if he were watching a tennis match, before he finally sighed and shook his head.

"Don't be difficult babe, not tonight, please. These are the only two choices, you know that."

She looked down at the deteriorating pages that were falling apart in her hands and had a second thought.

"How about tonight we come up with our own story? What do you think about that?"

She raised a persuasive eyebrow to her son whose excitement made it obvious he did not need much convincing. He took an unexpected dive under his blankets and when he resurfaced he was holding an old journal and a red crayon.

The journal had a scratched leather cover with three golden buttons that held the book closed. It used to be his mother's journal when she was young. It was a gift given with the intention that it would hold all of her hopes and dreams, to help her visualize her destiny, but now it was empty. She had torn all of the pages out of the journal that had housed the inspired words when she stopped believing in what she could become. His mother had forced herself to forget all that had been written.

She had given the remains to her son in hopes that one day he would have a dream of his own to manifest. After his mother had read to him, the boy would often stay up at night and stare into the journal, imagining words for a new story to fill the blank spaces.

"You are so weird," she said with admiration.

"Do you want a pencil, like a normal human being?"

He shook his head no, that he preferred his crayon, and waited eagerly for the story to begin.

"This is the story of a young boy who was born to be a hero, a boy just like you."

She tapped on her son's chest with her finger.

"His mission was to save people from sadness and he would use his special powers to help people find happiness. He would make everything all better and then he would search the world to find the next sad person who needed saving. This hero was a secret super hero because nobody knew his name, *but* everyone recognized him by his magical…"

The young mother paused to give her creativity a chance to catch up. Her son was staring up at her with expectant eyes.

"A magical…"

She scanned the room for inspiration and saw that her son was pointing up at her.

"A bandana?"

She lightly touched the red cloth that was covering her gash. The boy stuck his chin forward and bobbed his head.

"I like that, very original," she said, tightening the knot in the back of the bandana.

"Hey, you aren't writing any of this down!"

The boy looked down at his blank book in shock and put a death grip on his crayon. He furiously scribbled about two lines with his tongue sticking out of the corner of his mouth before pretending to be caught up. His mother tapped her chin and wrapped her fingers around a hopeful smile on her face.

"Does our story have a happy ending?"

The boy turned up his nose and shook his head.

"You are evil," she laughed, surprised by his guiltless depravity.

"So, what happens? How does it end? I guess he doesn't save the world?"

The boy shook his head concussively and waved his crayon back and forth in the air.

"He doesn't have to, you know. He doesn't have to save the world to be a hero. You know how many people you need to save to be a real hero?"

The boy looked down at his fingers and began calculating and computing the complex mathematics of heroism. He then held up all of his fingers as a rough guess. His mom reached forward and folded all but one finger back into his palm.

"Just one person. You can save just one person and be a hero, because you save their world," she reassured.

"Personally, if I get to vote, I think it should end with the boy coming home to his mama who loves him very much and missed him the whole time he was out there doing hero stuff. Make sure you write that down."

The boy moaned his disapproval.

"Oh, what, you are too cool for your mother now? Too big and strong, are you?"

She lunged towards him and grabbed his waist, flipping him upside down as he squealed at the top of his lungs.

"Help! Help! Who is going to save you? Who is going to save the boy with the bandana?"

As soon as the question left her mouth it demanded an answer.

A loud crash echoed through the house as the front door flew open and heavy footsteps followed. The young mother scrambled out of her son's bed and across the carpet to lock the door, flipping the light switch and engulfing the room in darkness. She sat with her back against the closet and picked up the knife off of the ground. She held it in front of her chest like a burning candle.

A hard hand began to hammer against the frame and drunken threats spilled through the hinges. The mother put her finger over her lips and begged her son, who was clutching the journal against his chest for protection, for silence. The steady blows began to wear down the old door frame which shuddered and splintered. The falling shards rained down like wooden confetti onto the carpet. Time froze on the moment before the door finally fell. The hands of the clock held on for dear life. There was a breathless silence. There was a deceptive peace. Then there was nothing at all.

Then came the final kick that shattered the door to pieces. Then came the raging man with the coiled belt. Then came the first blow to the boy's face, splitting open his cheek. Then came another. Then another.

The monstrous man wrapped his hand around the boy's fragile throat and the boy began to go numb. His arms went limp by his sides and one by one his senses started to shut down. There was a high pitched ringing in his ears and he could hear only the muted sounds of a shrill, animalistic scream followed by a deep howl. The grip on his throat loosened and he fell softly back onto his mattress. He lay there motionless, feeling the life pump slowly back into his chest. Out of the corner of his eye he saw a blur of movement on the floor. It was the shadow of his mother thrashing on top of the mountain of a man. Too weak to move, too weak to help, the boy rolled his eyes back to the ceiling and hoped for the nightmare to end. But as the silence came and he lay there in the middle of the madness, he knew that this was just the beginning of it.

Chapter 1: Imaginary Hero

He was the king of many castles and the slayer of dragons. He was whatever he believed himself to be, an imaginary hero saving the world inside his fantasy…

The rain fell mercilessly upon the disheartened knight as a storm raged through the haunted woods. Violent winds carried dark curses from the shadows as the obscure edges of the forest began to close in on the lonely path that he walked. The knight let his long iron sword fall to the ground behind him, dropped to a knee in the wet earth and pulled off his helmet to reveal his strong, slim face and amorphous, swirling irises. He tiredly pressed his back against the trunk of a giant dead tree that had been torched from the inside out. He looked to a tower that held a flickering light behind the peaks of silhouette mountains. It seemed that his daring quest of rescue would reach a disappointing end, defeated by the depression of the dark. He cast his gaze to the faint moon hiding behind the curtain of rain and contemplated the complexities of heroism.

For a decade he had searched for someone to save, just one person who would help him become a hero, a real hero, but to no avail. So he was lost, wandering within his imaginary walls, with nearly the entirety of his existence fictitious. His adventure, his purpose, his bravery – it was all pretend. He doubted if he could ever truly become who he always dreamed he was.

The boy scanned the sky and analyzed the vivid detail of his creation. He felt like an actor surrounded by the set of an ever-shifting stage. His mind was his only freedom, and although he chose to escape from the world often, he always felt a sense of pride in knowing how beautiful it could have been if he were to have created it.

The boy extended an open hand and watched the raindrops explode into his palm. He cupped his fingers and a puddle formed inside of his hand. He pointed up to the hidden moon and pulled it above his head to create a spotlight. He then carefully dotted the blank sky with constellations of stars and systems of planets in perfect ellipses. The boy angled his wrist towards the moon, tilted his hand, and leaned forward to see the reflection of the universe swimming slowly in the pool in his palm. He smiled at his cosmos as they danced in orbit, but it was only for a passing revolution before his planetary peace was interrupted.

There was a jarring, violent tremble that rattled the trees and quaked the earth below his feet. He let out a silent cry as his universe spilled between his shaking fingers and splashed onto the ground.

The blinking boy looked on in confusion at the chaos unfolding in front of him. He was standing in front of an overflowing sink in a small, decrepit bathroom with a puddle of soap dripping down his hand. Hot water poured over the edges of the stained basin and the boy lunged frantically to shut off the rusted faucet, burning his fingertips on the scorching metal handle. An angry set of knuckles rapped on the door and a shrill voice threatened consequences. The dying lightbulb dangling above his head buzzed and flickered spastically, setting a psychotic pace to the panic. The boy threw a towel onto the floor and tried to soak up the flood, while wiping at the steam on the broken mirror. A jagged piece of glass cut him cleanly beneath his thumb. He wrapped it in his white tee shirt to cover the sight of the blood. He leaned his elbows on the sink to steady himself and fight from fainting. He felt queasy, but catching a harrowing glimpse of himself in the mirror was even more unsettling. In the broken glass he saw a boy perpetually punished by chance. His face was an empty, hollow mask that hid him from his own presence, a lifeless mannequin, apathetic to his own misery. This is what he had become, or rather, this is what was left of him, after ten years of isolation in the foster home of 84 D.

The boy flicked off the light and snuck out of the bathroom into the narrow hallway, walking with his head down and his hands tucked into his shallow pockets. For all intents and purposes, the boy was living in a claustrophobic collectable lunchbox. The home was a living relic of Miss Jennie's childhood. The neurotically nostalgic foster parent was born, raised, and planned to die without ever having to change her address. The décor of the house was too tasteless to be labeled as vintage, and the overall ambiance was similar to that of an abandoned carnival. There were rooms full of torn open stuffed animals left for dead, unopened boxes of antique dolls with murderous blank stares stacked to the ceiling, plastic telephones flipped upside down on oval racetrack rugs and clusters of sprawling, polluted toy block cities. As if the aesthetic couldn't be worse imagined, every inch of the home was covered in depressing, grey, wilted flowered wallpaper.

As the boy made his way to his room he passed through the main exhibit of her museum of repressed trauma: the abstract animals gallery. Framed with shameless pride on the walls, was a collection of pencil drawings from Miss Jennie's most anatomically confused days as a child. Each picture was a disfigured version of some charismatic creature from the pasture with its features rearranged in the most scandalous of compositions for the sake of art. The boy's room was, unsurprisingly, just as outdated and awful. There was a splintered set of wooden bunk beds pushed into one corner and a pink race car bed parked in the other. A series of cartoon posters were hung across the walls and ceiling by long nails, with a discomforting pattern of placement through heads and hearts. An arching, crooked rainbow had been painted across the wallpaper of the widest wall of the room, but the colors had faded long ago. As had Miss Jennie's – a faded woman who had been put through the wash far too many times.

Miss Jennie believed that the past was perfect, and apparently current, as she refused to accept time's progression and declined to alter anything within her home. What was broken remained broken, preserved like an ancient artifact. She believed that nothing would ever be better than what it had been, so she refused to make a thing worse than it was. With an impressive display of self-control, she also abstained from altering her level of maturity, her wardrobe, or her incessant habit of chewing gum out of the corner of her mouth, for the better part of her life.

To constantly remind herself of how golden adolescence was, each night she locked herself in her room and re-watched her favorite home videos from when she was young projected onto the wall without sound. It was a painful and pitiful practice, often haunting the house with lonely laughs and cries in the aching hours of the night. Therefore, Miss Jennie was often out of sight and out of mind, leaving the children to fend for themselves. However, whenever there came an opportunity to inflict pain, physical or psychological, behind the guise of discipline, she was never absent. It would seem that she hated the children, partly because she wished she still was one. The truth behind her creative and cruel punishments she was infamous for was that she was desperate for a good laugh, coming inevitably at the expense of a child's terror. But even cheap laughs could not replenish the vibrancy her life had lost over the years. She had blended into her environment like a cynical chameleon. She had become a stereotype, a vile and vengeful cliché, after growing tired of laughing at all of life's sick jokes. She used to find humor in the chaos that she created in her youth, but once she lost control of the world's madness, she didn't find it all that funny anymore.

The boy slowed his steps as he walked past her closed door and leaned his ear in to listen. There was a thick mix of silence and muffled sniffling. The boy shook his head and crept into his room, closing the door quietly behind him. Lying on the floor at his feet was his lonely friend Leo. He had a flashlight tucked under his chin and was pinching a pair of loose electrical wires that had been pulled out of a mysterious hole in the base of the wall. He squinted in deep concentration as he touched the wires together, which created a massive spark that caused him to flinch dramatically. He wiped away a bead of sweat that had formed above his eyebrow and prepared for another trial. The boy with the colorful eyes crouched down to inspect the experiment and Leo handed off the flashlight.

"The light won't turn on. I think I can fix it. Hey, if I can figure out these wires maybe I can find a way to electrocute myself with them. I figure it would probably be the most exciting thing to happen to me all summer. It would be nice to have something to do, something to look forward to," he said, drying his sweaty palms on his pants.

"I would want it to really shock me though, not just tingle. I want to shut things down in there, you know?"

The boy with the colorful eyes handed the flashlight back to Leo. Showing far less interest in the effects of electrocution, the boy left him to his experiment and climbed up the rickety ladder of his bunk bed.

"It might give me superpowers, you never know. Or better yet, it could kill me instantly," he said.

Leo's use of dark humor was just one of his several coping mechanisms that he applied in order to compensate for his inability to accept the trauma that bludgeoned him throughout his life. Leo paired his humor with an infallible confidence in his own ability to solve the world's problems. Leo had many gifts, but he never had the opportunity to open them. He was extremely intelligent, personable and passionate. Leo was of the genius type, except without all of the twitchy tendencies that are to be expected from a character of that design. Leo was a cool person. He was genuine. He was a dreamer. He was a believer in every way and above all he believed in himself.

However, in many ways Leo had attributes that fit the genius mold – the first being his unique pair of glasses. They were unique due to the fact that they only had one lens. Leo had popped the other out of the frame because he wasn't using it. He was born partially blind in his left eye and wanted to champion the impairment rather than hide it behind false glass. Leo's attire also spoke to his character. He sported the same black sweatshirt with the NASA logo every single day despite the summer heat, and would alternate out his pants when he decided they were dirty.

Leo was a creature of scholarly habits and perpetually curious about obscurities, yet his defining feature was not his intellect, but rather his sensibility. He was a fragile human being with a delicate heart and a sentimental soul. He was easily flustered and lived at the cruel mercy of his emotions. Out of all the questions that he pondered, the 'why' is what ate away at him the most. He could never seem to find a justifiable reason for his misfortune, and the fates were far too arrogant to explain themselves.

Thus, Leo did not have control of the causes yet suffered from the effects. But he was not the only one caught within a ceaseless series of unfortunate events. As misery loves company, the day he was delivered to the doorstep of 84 D ten years ago, he met his one and only companion. Best friends by default, he and the boy with the spinning eyes shared a crucial, unspoken bond in the most literal sense of the word.

The mute boy in the bunk bed tucked his legs under his thin blanket and pulled back the tattered cloth from the tilted, triangular window. He propped up his pillow behind him and looked out at the lonely home across the street. There were only two houses left in the forsaken neighborhood that sat encroaching on the edge of a sprawling industrial city. When the machinery moved in, suburbia moved out, but 84 D's roots were rotted beneath the ground. Thus, it was fitting that the boy felt buried alive at the border of a dead end street.

In the sole home on the other side of the road, there was a window directly across from his own. In that window there was a teenage girl laying in her bed with a book open in front of her, working her strawberry blonde hair into a long braid. The boy assumed that she was close to his age of fifteen, but her vibrant aesthetic portrayed her as younger than she was. The girl lazily flipped the page she was reading and folded its corner to mark her place before pushing away the book and rolling onto her side to face the window. Her vacant eyes seemed to simultaneously scan the night sky for both something specific and for nothing at all. The boy followed her gaze but knew that his would not be met; she had never once looked in his direction. The girl rolled over on her back and crossed her hands in her lap, staring up at the ceiling fan and watching it spin. Every now and again she would take a sour glance at the clock and sigh. The boy knew what she was waiting for. It was the same thing she waited for every night.

Suddenly, the girl bounced up and scrambled onto the floor, diving under her bed. She clumsily crawled out from below holding a pink corded telephone that was hidden beneath a sheet. She watched it ring anxiously, counting down the socially required waiting time, then yanked it off the hook and answered with a yawn. She lay with her back on the floor and crossed her feet up on her bed, twirling the cord in her long fingers and mindlessly wrapping it around her arms.

An unexpected knock at the door put an immediate end to her secret conversation. She was forced to quickly untangle herself from the knotted cord and shove the phone back beneath the bed. She flipped the book off of the mattress and onto the floor next to her, and then stuck a pencil behind her ear. A middle-aged woman wearing blue nursing scrubs pushed the door open with her foot and held out a tub of ice cream with two spoons stabbed into it like mythical swords. Her daughter clapped and kicked the book to the side as her mother dropped down next to her on the carpeted floor. The two traded animated stories as they exchanged frozen scoops. The girl laid her head in her mother's lap and waved her spoon around as she spoke. Her mother began to delicately unwind her daughter's twisted hair and run her fingers through it. A few moments later the father joined them, kissing both of his girls on the tops of their heads and resting his own on his wife's shoulder. He vied for their attention as he told what the watching boy assumed to be an old, recycled dad joke and they all laughed in perfect unison. The boy in the window would have laughed too, if he could have heard what was said.

The boy knew that he was watching something special, or perhaps it was normal, but to him it was special because his normal was anything but special. He had observed the family across the sidewalks for many years while trapped in his tower. The boy served as an invisible witness to the potential of love's versatility and durability, despite his concept of family being fractured and nearly forgotten. He had difficulties remembering vivid details of his mother or of the night that took her from him. All he knew was that he had been loved and that he was meant to be a hero, but as time wore away at the memories he was left not truly understanding what either of those things meant.

The boy liked to imagine that he was a part of the perfect family that lived on the other side of the window, but every night when the lights went off and he was stuck staring at the darkness from the outside, he was reminded that he most certainly was not.

Chapter 2: Flame Faces

The boy thrashed from side to side as he clawed at his eyes to try and stop the burning. Tears singed his face like dripping acid and he coughed until his ribs rattled. He folded himself in half as his sweaty lips searched for air to breathe.

The boy reached blindly for the window and pried open the jammed frame. He sucked at the oxygen from the outside, pulling his shirt off over his head and tying it around his face. The room around him had become a noxious cloud of dense black smoke. Acrobatic flames jumped through the darkness and the painted rainbow wall melted theatrically in front of him. Leo crawled beneath the billowing smoke across the burning carpet, dragging a shoebox behind him. The sprinkler head looked on indifferently from the ceiling above, poised with the perfect view to watch the boys burn alive.

"I fell asleep! I don't know what happened," Leo called out over the roar of the fire as he cowered in the corner.

"It can't end like this, we have to get out of here," he cried, his agonized voice muffled by the sharp cracking of burning wood.

The boy in his bunk untied a pair of sneakers that were hanging by their laces from the bed post. He grabbed the left one by the heel and flung it at the dormant sprinkler head but missed the target. The errant shoe flew into the wall and landed sideways in a patch of flames. The boy refocused, steadied himself with his foot on the ladder and reached out to try and knock the sprinkler head with the other sneaker. He swung his arm and lost his balance, tumbling onto the floor with the ladder crashing down on top of him. The boy tried to scramble to the door, swatting wildly at the approaching flames but was met with sweltering resistance. He retreated into a small space between the bunk bed and the corner of the wall and waited there.

"Somebody help us!" Leo screamed towards the window.

Leo's panicked eyes snapped to the boy across the room who was staring at him with an unexpected stillness. A strange, almost peaceful silence followed. Their fear seemed to falter momentarily as they looked on in awe at the inferno in front of them. There was something curiously calming about watching the wall burn, and something oddly empowering about not trying to fight it. The boy considered that this may be some sort of symbol – a metaphor of destruction or wrath – or perhaps it was only what it was – a house burning to the ground. The boy felt selfish for attempting to dissect meaning from the chaos.

The longer he watched the fire dance the more entranced he became and the less he cared to escape. A dangerous apathy settled in. He began to see faces in the flames, flickering figures that morphed into distorted portraits. The boy believed he saw his own reflection glowing back at him, but the face was both more and less than his own. He recognized features that were not his, but he felt that he knew who they belonged to. Before he could be sure, the face split into two and vanished.

As it did, the bedroom door swung open and a wave of white foam flooded the room and suffocated the flames. When the fire was finally choked out, a sweaty Miss Jennie stood in the center of the room with an unwieldy metal extinguisher in her hands and an empty canister at her feet. She wiped off her red polka-dotted dress and scanned the room skeptically. Her eyes first jumped to the sprinkler head that seemed to ignore her, and then they traced the roasted rainbow in a suspicious arc down to the tangled set of electrical wires protruding from the wall. She crouched down and examined them closely as the distant sound of sirens rang in from the window. She stood slowly and turned to the boys, making clear and direct eye contact with one and then the other.

"Well played," she said, snapping her over-chewed gum out of the corner of her pursed lips.

She turned on her heel abruptly and exited, closing the door delicately behind her. It was in that merciful moment that both of the boys wondered if they had really been saved.

***

"So, you like to play with fire?"

Miss Jennie sat on a tall, skinny stool with her legs crossed tightly. She callously put the finishing touches of nail polish on the ends of her primped fingers while snapping her gum at the boys kneeling on the kitchen floor in front of her. There was a plethora of props collected next to them that all seemed to be loosely related to the boys' impending punishment. There was a pile of winter clothes, a large wax candle, two boxes of short matches and a metal garbage can assembled in a straight line. The boys surveyed the selection distrustfully, but honestly it wasn't the strangest they had come across. It had been over a week since they turned their room into a toaster and they had been patiently awaiting their consequence as Miss Jennie plotted.

Not only did they charcoal her childhood bedroom, they also set her up for some serious backlash from the fire marshal for an array of safety violations. Thus, they expected her worst, but lately her worst wasn't all that bad. Miss Jennie's fear tactics lost most of their power when the other foster children were adopted, and now with just the two strange boys left to torture, it seemed to take some of the fun out of it for her. The boys could sense her lack of commitment and decided to treat their punishment like a performance where all they had to do was just play their parts to make it through the show.

"Good to know," she responded to the silence.

"Let's get this over with. Being around you two is already unbearable. This is going to be an experiment because every time I tried to think of a way to make you two suffer the only idea that made me happy was setting you both on fire, but that is basically why we are here in the first place. I was afraid you would enjoy it, which forces me to be a little more creative, and honestly, you don't deserve the effort."

The two boys nodded in unison.

"I have a few different fire drills prepared for you," she said, leaving space for a reaction at the end of her sentence.

Leo rolled his eyes at her cheap play on words, just like she wanted him to. Leo knew she was fishing for a response, so he decided to bite the bait.

"I will rip them out of your head," Miss Jennie threatened with a satisfied smile.

Miss Jennie disliked everyone pretty much equally, but she harbored a special hatred for Leo. She had always been deeply offended by his infinite solutions to the problems she created for him. She had made her living snatching souls from the dejected children that had passed through her halls, but Leo had a spirit that could not be stolen, making her lust for it more than anything.

"That pun was part of the punishment," she continued, sitting up obnoxiously straight in her stool, "Now, put on all of those winter clothes until you overheat and pass out."

Miss Jennie pointed her wet nail to the assortment of jackets and scarves heaped on the floor. She rolled the end of her stretched gum in her fingertips and waited.

The boys idly sorted through the pile of gear and shot each other suspicious looks. Miss Jennie's punishments were typically respected for their genius in their simplicity and wickedness, but this one seemed desperate and contrived. Miss Jennie's cruelty was one of her last defining features and the boys could not imagine who she would be without it. For so many years they had grown accustomed to fearing her; it was a symbiotic relationship between predator and prey, but now that they were not afraid of her they almost didn't know how to act.

The boys tried to cooperate but her punishment was too poorly conceived. The winter clothes that had been collected did not belong to them; they were leftovers from other foster children who had been lucky enough to escape. They were all too small to even try on. Their arms became stuck in the sleeves and they didn't bother forcing the issue. Once Miss Jennie realized that her first attempt was a failure, she proceeded with her second castigation which was arguably less successful than her first. She ordered the boys to each take a box of matches and light them one by one, letting them burn out on their fingertips. In theory, it sounded tortuous, but in reality it was only slightly uncomfortable.

Miss Jennie's penultimate punishment forced the boys to take turns holding the wax candle as it melted and dripped onto their hands. In principle, one was supposed to suffer until they could no longer endure and then pass the pain off to their partner in crime. It would pin them against each other, breaking their will and tearing apart their friendship. To Miss Jennie's credit it was sadistic enough to work, except that both of the boys secretly enjoyed the sensation of the melting wax and impatiently waited for their turn to hold the candle once more.

Miss Jennie looked on at her failed punishments impassively, twirling an extra matchstick in her fingers.

"I guess you guys will never learn your lesson." She shrugged, blowing on the ends of her freshly painted nails.

"Should we go to our room?" Leo asked, leaning down the hallway.

Miss Jennie nodded with a counterfeit smile.

"Just don't enjoy yourselves in there," she said, holding her hand up to admire her work.

"We won't," Leo promised.

Leo and the boy turned to walk away when they heard the sizzling strike of a match. Miss Jennie posed next to the garbage can holding up the lid and dangling the flame over the opening.

"Oh yeah, one last thing… It's only fair, if you burn my memories, I burn yours. It isn't a punishment, it's justice," she said, letting the match fall and slamming down the lid.

"Just justice," she repeated.

Miss Jennie walked off to her room, bumping into Leo who rushed past her to the garbage can. He rashly lifted the lid and stuck his arm inside but yanked it away as his hand was greeted by the heat. Leo stepped to the side and flipped over the bin, emptying the flaming contents onto the middle of the kitchen floor. The boy watched on anxiously at a distance as Leo stomped out the smoldering fire. After the last flame had been suffocated, Leo began to rummage through the charred collection of their belongings.

The boy could see his two coverless picture books burnt from front to back, as well as his cherished action figure whose face was now a smear of melted plastic. Leo recovered a few of his precious childhood photos that now had singed edges and put them back in his special box that Miss Jennie had emptied and dumped into the garbage. Leo crouched down and examined the plastic bottle of nail polish remover that had been used to douse their belongings. He shook his head and flung the bottle into the toppled garbage can. Leo squinted his good eye at a pile of smoking papers that had stuck to the bottom of the can. As he peeked his head inside, his voice bounced back over his shoulder, "It didn't burn," he said, pinching at the corner of a buried cloth.

Leo pulled himself out of the trash and shook off the boy's red bandana which was covered in a thin layer of ash. The boy quickly shoved the bandana into his back pocket both grateful and embarrassed. His mother had slipped it off of her head and into his backpack moments before the police came to take her away. The boy tied it around his head the day he first arrived at the foster home and he wore it for years without ever taking it off. Then, one day when he was watching the family from the window, he had the seeping sensation that his mother was never coming back. So, he untied the bandana and buried it in his backpack where it would live for years.

"I can't believe I almost burned her house down…we were so close," Leo sighed, and then surprised himself by laughing.

"Back to the drawing board."

The two boys stepped into the bathroom to wash off the dried wax left over from their pyro punishments, and took turns running their arms beneath the sink. Typically, neither of the boys was ever deeply affected by Miss Jennie's drastic scare tactics. Her desperation was a sign that they were winning the war and needed to keep fighting the good fight, but Miss Jennie had taken a cheap shot. She had changed the game. Her retaliation was malicious and personal. Miss Jennie didn't just want to punish them, she wanted to hurt them and give them new scars. Leo flipped down the toilet seat and sat to contemplate.

"Now that I think about it, I'm pretty sure that half of the stuff she does to us is illegal. More than half. Much more than half actually. Basically everything she has done has broken some type of law."

Leo rested his arms back on the toilet tank.

"The old Miss Jennie was worse though… or I guess I should say the younger Miss Jennie. I think *that* Miss Jennie actually wanted to kill us. I almost feel bad for this new Miss Jennie. This Miss Jennie is a bit pathetic. I know that she means well… actually she means the opposite of well for us but she just isn't good at it anymore. You understand what I am saying?"

The boy rinsing his hands nodded, scraping away at a stubborn patch of wax.

"I have always respected the audacity of her creativity though. She really goes for it. Do you remember when she tried to give us rabies by telling us that those two stray dogs were our new pets? She even gave them fake names to make them seem friendlier."

The boy remembered it all too well.

"Or how about when she tried to get us arrested for shoplifting by telling us that the dressing rooms were outside? That woman locked us in a closet and made us peel onions with our bare hands to punish us for not crying at the ending of her favorite movie and it was animated."

The boy's focus began to fade into a flashback but Leo saw his attention slipping and waved his hand to bring the boy's mind back.

"It's funny but it's not. That woman has done horrible things to us – things that are not okay. I hate this place. I mean I really hate this place. When they brought us here, did you ever imagine that after all this time we would still be here? Why are we still here? Why are we the only ones left? What did we do?"

There was no answer. There was nothing to be said and the silent boy who only listened was the perfect person not to say it. Leo was right. Leo was rarely wrong. Even in Leo's moments of frightening vulnerability there was always truth in his hysterics.

"We don't deserve this, nobody deserves this. When I thought that fire was going to kill us I was not scared of burning alive, I was scared of dying here. We need to get out of this place, no matter what it takes. I don't care what I have to do."

Leo flicked off the bathroom light with finality and led them to their room, each of them dropping obscene hand gestures at Miss Jennie's doorstep as they passed by.

The boy climbed up to his bed and checked at the foot of his blanket to make sure his hidden journal was still concealed. Miss Jennie had missed it. He hadn't written much in it over the years, just a few feeble attempts at creating a story out of nothing, but he hoped that one day he would have a tale worth telling. Whether he would ever fill it or not, it did not deserve to burn.

Leo reached up from his bunk below and handed up a book that the silent boy kept under his bed. He stretched out his legs and opened up his own book to the page with the folded corner. The two boys loved to read. They shared a passion for stories but never would share one. Leo read only non-fiction, true events that were wrapped in reality, whereas the boy immersed himself in the fictitious. Leo wanted to read about only what had been done, thought, and said in the true story of the world, whereas the boy did not have a strict philosophy. He just preferred to be in the pretend.

"I can't concentrate," Leo called out, closing his book.

"Is it cool if I come up?" he asked, already half way up the ladder of the bunk bed. The boy slid over to make room on the undersized mattress and pulled back the window curtain. It was time to tune in to their regularly scheduled program: the reality show that aired across the street. There was never any sound or subtitles, so the boys had to make due with context clues and solid acting performances.

"Tonight must be the night," Leo speculated.

"She looks nervous."

The strawberry haired daughter was pacing back and forth in the kitchen, twirling the small pearls of her necklace anxiously with her fingertips. The lights in the dining room were dimmed, the table was set with fine silverware, and her parents were huddled around the stove putting the finishing touches on the evening's dishes. Each time that the daughter caught a glimpse of her reflection she stopped to assess herself. Her hair was held back neatly by a light green headband and in each ear dangled a jeweled pink flamingo. The girl's white dress was playfully patterned with palm trees and blue waters and she twisted it from side to side. The girl rushed to the mirror and put on her glasses, took them off, then put them on again, before ultimately shoving them in a drawer.

"We knew this day would come. The boyfriend is finally coming over for the first time to meet the parents," Leo gauged.

The boy next to him shook his head in disagreement.

"No? Are you trying to be technical? If it isn't her official boyfriend then it is her secret boyfriend who she says is just a friend."

The boy gave a half shrug and rubbed his chin.

"You don't think the parents know about her mystery phone friend? She isn't as sneaky as she thinks she is. It has to be him."

The boy rocked back pensively against his pillow.

"I can't guess your fan theory. I don't know what you think you are seeing but I know what I am seeing. I guarantee you that someone comes knocking on that door…"

As Leo spoke the words an unexpected knock came at their own door. It was an unusually polite and permission seeking tap. A gentle voice called out from the other side and the handle turned slowly. The boys braced themselves as the door delicately swung open and a stranger stepped into their world. Standing in the doorway, wrapped in mystery, was the shadowy silhouette of a girl and her suitcase.

Chapter 3: Elle Lavender's Energy

The effervescence of the mystical girl lit the dark room like a sunrise. She radiated boldly, with her beaming smile burning its image into the back of the boys' eyelids when they blinked. The girl had a quirky, skinny frame covered by a white, short-sleeved collared shirt snuck under a velvet dress. The girl's lanky legs were tucked into a pair of untied sneakers from which she had stolen the laces to tie up her restless ombre curls on top of her head. The girl's smooth, caramel skin was spotted with amber freckles and her magnetic eyes borrowed blue from the sky and a splash of green from the sea.

The mystifying stranger stood patiently with her arms behind her back in the middle of the charred room next to her white suitcase. She curiously examined what was left of the singed wall behind her while tapping one foot on top of the other. The two boys watched her suspiciously from the safety of their bunk bed as she roamed around their chamber. The girl graciously waved at the boys and they awkwardly waved back to her. She then took a hesitant step towards them, raising her eyebrow as she did, before gliding across the floor and up their ladder in one fluid movement. She sat herself on the end of the bed facing them and extended her hand.

"Elle Lavender," she said, blinking at the boy with the colored eyes.

That boy would never forget how she introduced herself that day – as if Elle Lavender was not just a name she had been given, but was the definition of who she was.

"And you are?" she asked.

"Leo," Leo interjected and put his clammy hand in hers.

"My full name is Leonid."

"That's fun," she said, turning her head back to the silent boy, who, always true to his word, said nothing.

"And what do you call him?" Elle Lavender asked.

"I…" Leo started to respond but glued the answer to his lips as the boy with the colorful eyes waved him to a stop.

"I don't think he likes his name. He never used to respond to it," Leo said.

Elle raised one eyebrow perilously high.

"So who are you then? Just a boy?" Elle Lavender challenged.

The boy pulled his eyes away from the girl's lulling stare.

Elle shrugged with a friendly indifference and took his hand in hers. "Well, it's a pleasure to meet you, Boy."

Boy let her fingers fall out of his hand as if he were trying to catch water.

"Do you both sleep in this bed?" she asked bluntly, eying the empty bed below them.

"No, I sleep down there, we just come up here to watch the family across the street," Leo answered, tossing a thumb over his shoulder towards the window.

Elle placed a pause on the conversation to give herself a chance to reinterpret what had been said.

"Did that feel comfortable saying out loud?" she asked.

"Honestly, no," Leo said, sliding the tattered curtain closed.

Elle gave Leo a light punch in the shoulder.

"It looks like I need to find a place to sleep," she said.

Leo's eyes hinted to the pink race car bed in the corner of the room. Elle followed his gaze but windshield-wiped her finger back and forth.

"Oh no. It's *really* not my color."

The bed-less girl held the unflinching stare of the bed-rich boy as they held their breath. Elle nodded her head imperceptibly towards the race car, and Leo shook his head ever so slightly. This time, Elle gave a flex of her skinny arm and guided Leo to the bed once more with an even more subtle tilt of the head.

The standoff had been won.

"It's actually not that bad once you get used to it," Leo called out from the driver seat of the car, lying with his legs popping out of the trunk.

Elle Lavender laid on her back in her newly gifted bed, with her feet pressed into the bottom of Boy's mattress above her.

"I'm just glad it's a convertible," Leo said.

Boy put his arms behind his head and dropped snugly down into his pillow. There was electricity in the silence that followed. There was a current coursing through the room that made them restless. A static was in the air that they shared and there was no question as to who the energy was flowing from.

"Sweet dreams, my friends. Happy to be here," Elle Lavender whispered from the darkness.

Boy rolled over onto his side and closed his eyes lightly. For the first time in his entire life, he too was happy to be there.

***

The fusing colors of Boy's eyes slowly separated and the blurry form in front of him revealed itself to be Elle Lavender eating cereal from a plastic bowl. She sat directly in front of Boy in his bed with her legs crossed, stabbing the prongs of her fork through the fruit flavored loops. She munched coolly, watching Boy as he returned from his fantasy. A mutinous piece of cereal flung onto his leg and Elle reached over, scooped it up, and ate it without apologies. She raised the bowl to her mouth and drank the leftover milk while she watched him out of the corner of her eye.

"Does it hurt when your eyes do that?" she asked, using her long fingers to reenact the splitting of Boy's colors.

Boy shook his head.

"I like that you don't talk," she said, using the back of her hand to wipe away the milk mustache that had formed on the top of her lip.

"I am too young to have already heard so many people say so many words."

She threw Boy a smooth wink and climbed down the ladder with the plastic fork stabbed into her mouth.

Once the boys were fully awake they gathered with Elle in the center of the room, each pulling over one of Miss Jennie's old forgotten toys to use as a seat. Elle mounted a wooden rocking horse that wobbled more from side to side than front to back, Leo straddled the head of a long plastic caterpillar that taught the alphabet, and Boy stole a chair from the miniature tea party table. Elle rolled over her suitcase, pulled out three lollipops and handed them out to the group.

"Where did you get these?" Leo asked.

"From my suitcase," Elle answered.

"You just wheel around lollipops in your suitcase?"

"I wheel around a lot of things in my suitcase."

Boy grimaced as the hard candy knocked against his teeth.

"There is a piece of gum trapped in the middle, so whatever you do, don't quit," Elle said.

The crew was silently savoring their lollipops when Elle noticed Boy's shoes that had been burned in the fire.

"You must be pretty fast," she said.

Boy rubbed his thumb on his singed sneakers.

"We should race sometime."

Elle stuck the lollipop in the corner of her mouth and pointed her elbow at the melted rainbow wall.

"I like what you guys have done with the place."

"I started a fire," Leo said.

"Accidentally," Elle added for clarity.

"Accidentally," Leo echoed shortly.

"Do you like to start fires?"

"Can't say I do."

"You should say you don't. Then again, it's nice to have hobbies," Elle said with her lollipop bulging in the corner of her cheek.

"I was experimenting with some wires and I fell asleep," Leo confessed.

"Boring experiment? Most are. You a scientist?" Elle asked.

"No," Leo admitted, "I am just a curious person."

Elle's eyes widened, "I hear that curiosity kills."

"Curiosity kills *cats*," Leo corrected.

"At least they have nine lives. We don't," Elle stuck her foot out and gave Leo a playful kick.

"You all should know that I am a poet," she announced, "I wouldn't want you to find out from someone else."

"Have you written any poems?" Leo asked skeptically.

"Aspiring poet."

"I see."

"I memorize poems that I like and reference them relentlessly."

"Tell us a poem then."

Elle shook her head.

"I'm not a vending machine. I don't dispense poetry on command."

Elle rocked herself slowly and proudly on the wooden horse.

"That's not the first time you've said that line," Leo said.

"And it won't be the last," Elle promised.

"You are young, younger than us anyways," Leo observed outwardly.

"Yes, but I am wise beyond your years," Elle said.

"You mean wise beyond *your* years."

"No, yours too."

The two boys secretly studied their new friend as she bit down aggressively on her lollipop and cracked the candy into sugary shards with her teeth. Her mannerisms were uncanny yet captivating. The way she spoke, the way she moved, even her impeccable posture was peculiar. She was so unique that it almost made Boy feel guilty that she was now a prisoner amongst them. However, the casual confidence that Elle Lavender exuded conveyed that she had no use for anyone's sympathy.

"How about we go around the circle and say something interesting about ourselves, so that we can get to know each other better?" Elle suggested.

"Technically, with three people we aren't a circle. We are more like a misshapen triangle," Leo corrected.

"Is that your interesting fact you would like to share?" Elle asked, pointing at Leo with her two index fingers pressed together.

"No, just an observation," Leo said.

"Then please wait your turn, we don't want to interrupt Boy."

They turned to Boy who conclusively said nothing.

"Enlightening. Thank you, Boy," Elle said, nodding thoughtfully.

"Anything to add?" Elle addressed Leo.

"My interesting fact is that I am blind in my left eye. I have been my whole life. It doesn't bother me and it doesn't slow me down, even with things like reading. You would think I could only read half as fast as people with normal vision but…"

"I actually wouldn't assume it would be such a simple conversion," Elle interrupted. "To be honest I was only wondering if you see nothing at all or if everything is just floating blurry shapes like a dying lava lamp," Elle said, letting the stick of the lollipop hang off her lips like a lit cigarette.

"It's all dark," Leo said.

"Are you afraid of the dark?" Elle asked.

"No, I don't see a reason to be," Leo said.

"You don't even see half a reason to be?" Elle snorted, waving the joke out of the air with her hand. "I'm sorry."

Leo surrendered a smile. He couldn't even be offended if he wanted to. Elle's eccentricity was laced with obvious innocence.

"I used to be afraid of the dark, until one day I wasn't. I want to tell you about that day," Elle said, scooching closer to the boys and poising herself to share a story. She tilted forward on her rocking horse and crossed one arm over the other. The two boys leaned in to meet her words halfway.

"When I was little, my parents and I would fly down once a year to visit my grandmother in the islands. She lived in a small wooden house on the edge of the beach. You could see the ocean from the kitchen. It was one of the most beautiful places in the world – during the day, I should say, because at night it turned into a land of horror. I would lie in bed listening to the noises outside the walls, and see the shadows waiting for me outside of my window. There were times when the breeze would push the front door open and you could hear the sound of the waves eating each other alive in the sea. I was so afraid that I would try to force myself to sleep during the day because I was too scared to close my eyes at night. When it was time for bed I would cry and beg my grandma not to leave the room. I thought that all the bad things came out when the sun went down. My grandma is the old school type, she didn't play any games, so after I complained one night she told me…" Elle screwed up her face and mimicked the raspy accent of her grandmother, "'…Ya crazy girl, you know nothin'. There ain't no such thing as darkness; we are just standing in the shade, baby. The sun don't ever stop shinin' not for a second no. It's always shinin' somewhere. So, ya just wait for it to come back around or ya give it a lil' chase if ya need to find it.'"

Elle sat so far forward on her rocking horse that the mouth was nearly kissing the ground.

"She told me if I needed the sun so bad I should go and find it. So, I did. After dinner, when the stars came out, I snuck out of the house and spent the whole night searching for the sunshine. I looked everywhere I could think that it might have been hiding. The noises were so loud and scary that I picked up a long stick and tucked it into my shorts in case I needed to fight somebody. The islands were a crazy place, you just never knew."

Elle paused her story to crack her neck. She used her knuckles to push her chin from side to side, stretched her arms out behind her back and then resumed.

"I checked behind the trees, I dug under the sand, I even went into the ocean thinking the sun might be holding its breath underwater. By the time I gave up it was already morning and I was soaking wet and shivery. I had to walk across almost the entire island to get back home and when I did my grandma was waiting for me outside. She grabbed me by the ear and screamed, 'What was ya thinkin' child?' She was furious. So I pointed to the sun that was just starting to rise and said, 'I found it!' Then she smacked me in the back of the head and told me I was going to get myself killed. So I said, 'Ya crazy girl, ya know nothing!', and she smacked me again."

An unexpected tear dropped down Elle's cheek.

"That's one of my favorite stories."

She wiped the tear away without any consideration.

"That happens sometimes," she said, showing off her sparkling smile.

"Have you ever gone swimming at night?" Elle asked.

Boy, who was fixated on the tear stain on Elle's cheek, absently shook his head and passed the question off to Leo with his eyes.

"I can't swim," Leo said.

"Well, then you definitely shouldn't swim at night."

Elle rose from her seat and wandered aimlessly around the room.

"Do you guys have any bicycles that I can borrow?"

"For what?"

"To ride. I'm not sure what else you would do with a bicycle," Elle said.

"Ride where?" Leo asked.

"Anywhere. Preferably everywhere. Do you have any?"

"No."

"Do you know how to ride a bike?"

"I understand the concept of how riding a bike works, but I've never ridden one," Leo admitted.

"I used to ride my bicycle every day in the summer growing up. There weren't many safe places to ride it so I basically rode in big circles around my neighborhood until I ended up back in my driveway. I would try not to ever use the brakes and sometimes I would even take both hands off the handlebars."

The two listening boys gave each other subtle, impressed nods.

"One day I found this place called 'The New Road', or at least I called it that, which I now admit wasn't very creative, but it was a brand new road that came out of nowhere. One summer it wasn't there and the next it was. I was doing my laps around the neighborhood when I saw it. I rode up the street and I saw they were building new houses up there, big ones, rich people houses that didn't belong with the rest of ours. Every single house on the entire street looked exactly the same. There was no originality. It was tragic. If I had built those houses I would have given them some imagination. I would have made each one special, so special you couldn't just ride your bike past them, you would have to stop and admire each one. They were building them up in the hills, basically on top of the city, and when I rode up there, I could see everything. It wasn't a beautiful view. It was sad actually."

Elle tucked her hands beneath her armpits.

"The New Road was the longest road I had ever been on. Maybe it is the longest of all time, I would have to ask around to confirm. At the end of the street was the longest driveway in the world. You couldn't even see the whole thing. I don't know if there was a house waiting at the end of that driveway. If there wasn't, then why build the driveway? If there was, why build the house so far away from the others? I never made it to the end of that driveway because I would have never made it back home in time before the street lights went out, no matter how fast I pedaled. Every day I wonder where that driveway leads to, but I will never know."

Boy watched the mysterious driveway unravel in his mind. He felt cheated that he didn't know where it ended.

"Riding a bike is…the best. We should go for a ride one day."

"We don't have any bicycles," Leo reminded her regretfully.

"Oh, yeah," Elle sighed and then quickly reanimated.

"Well, what do you guys like to do for fun around here? Besides, you know, arson?" Elle nodded at the wall for reference.

"There is nothing for us to do here, but I have big dreams for when I am out of here."

"What do you dream?" Elle asked, and then threw her eyes to floor and interrupted her own question by whispering to herself, "What a beautiful question."

Leo straightened up in his seat, "I dream of going to space with my father one day."

"Is that so?"

"He was training to be an astronaut before I came here and he promised he would take me."

"An astronaut and a scientist, quite an ambitious family," Elle said.

"My mom died when I was young and my dad couldn't raise me on his own. He needed to focus on his career," Leo said.

"That's heavy," Elle said, puffing up her cheeks and blowing out air.

"And what do you dream, Boy?" Elle asked.

Boy dreamed of everything and yet of only one thing. He thought of his hidden journal that housed his hero's tale. He could not explain what he dreamed. Even if she could have read his mind, his convoluted thoughts would need to be translated.

"What do you love, Elle?" Leo asked, pulling the half-eaten lollipop from his lips.

"Do you love telling your stories?"

"No," Elle said, her eyes levitating towards the window.

"I love to live them."

Elle dismounted the rocking horse with an elegant swing of her leg and then patted down her purple dress.

"Both of your dreams will come true," she guaranteed.

She turned and pointed her long finger on the end of her long arm at Leo.

"You will go to space with your father."

She whirled her prophetic finger to Boy.

"And you will do whatever you dream of doing."

Elle let her arm linger in the air.

"When are we going to start chasing our dreams?"

"They won't come true in here," Leo said, pinching the end of the lollipop between his teeth.

"We have to get out of here first before we start chasing them."

Elle scrunched her face and scratched the side of her head.

"The door isn't locked."

"We aren't free in here."

"You aren't trapped in here either," Elle offered with an anarchic shrug.

She let her turbulent words thrash around while she surveyed what remained of the cartoon posters that hung on the walls and ceiling.

"I am going to try and make the most of all this. I want to love it here, but maybe that's easy for me to say because I won't be here long," she said.

"That is what we all said," Leo crossed his arms defensively across his chest.

Elle folded her arms behind her back.

"But I am actually leaving," she spoke to the burnt poster in front of her face.

"I have been adopted before. The family is going through a tough time right now and couldn't afford to take care of me anymore. They had no choice but to give me up. They promised to come back for me."

"What happened to your real family?" Leo probed.

"They were real family."

"You know what I mean," Leo said.

"I prefer to leave the past in the past. I don't want to bring it back to life."

Elle turned around and her face was covered by a large bubble that she had blown with the piece of gum from the center of her lollipop. Boy tried to blow a bubble of his own but it came out dainty and misshapen, whereas Leo's piece fell out of his mouth and plopped directly on the ground. They all stared at the fallen gum that had been chewed up and spit out in solemn silence.

"I feel sad," Elle announced.

The two boys, not knowing what to do with this new information, continued to stare at the discarded gum that was stuck to the carpet.

"I am going to go cry in the bathroom if anyone would like to join me."

Boy raised his hand tentatively to the unusual invitation, but Elle had already left the room. He reached down and scooped the piece of gum off of the ground and handed it back to Leo on his way to the bathroom.

***

Elle sat on the end of the rusted tub with her elbows on her knees and her head hanging over the half-filled bath. Boy leaned his back against the front of the chipped toilet with his legs stretched across the tiled floor, his eyes cast down. The flickering light dangling above their heads surged in between the lonely sounds of dripping water and Elle's quiet sobs. Boy fidgeted uneasily as she cried thick, profound tears into the bath. Her suffering sent ripples through the basin, small waves of her past crashing against the shores of the tub. She wept steadily, genuinely, with her fingers trembling and her ribs aching, tears streaking down her face like rain on a windowpane. Elle cried until she was empty, then cupped warm water from the bath and splashed her face. She meditated for a moment before pulling the plug of the tub, holding the chain loosely and watching her pain swirl down the drain.

"Did you know that I've seen someone drown before?" she said, balancing herself on the edge of the bathtub.

"It was on my grandma's island a long time ago. There was a tourist who was swimming alone, splashing around and diving under the waves. He didn't know the waters well and wandered into a riptide," Elle said, sliding herself onto the floor, her eyes wide with forbidden intrigue.

"The man panicked, and tried to fight against the pull of the water, screaming and flailing the whole time, but nobody could help him. Everyone gathered on the beach to watch him struggle until his body quit and he sank. He washed up on the sand about an hour later, dead as you can be."

Elle spoke with a morbid calmness.

"He should have just let the current take him. The water around you can't kill you. He could have floated in the ocean for hours surrounded by all of the water in the world and nothing would have happened to him. The water is only dangerous if it gets trapped inside of you. Now, that is when you should panic."

Elle tapped the side of her head.

"Think about it."

Elle crawled forward and grabbed Boy's neck without warning. She pressed in slightly and began to take his pulse. She counted the measured beats under her breath and then placed her open palm on top of Boy's heart and squeezed her eyes shut.

"I feel like we have a connection," she said after finishing her vitals check.

"What do you think?" She forced Boy's hand across her own chest and spread his fingers out.

"Anything?"

He nodded. Boy didn't know what it was that he was feeling, but he was feeling it.

Elle's finger shot into the air.

"I know how to prove we are connected."

She jumped to her feet and pulled Boy up roughly behind her.

"Do you know your way around the city?"

Boy shook his head.

"Perfect."

***

Elle and Boy stood side by side in front of a labyrinth of narrow, crossing alleyways that dissected the heart of the industrial city. The thick, smog-filled air cast a daunting feeling of emptiness across the streets as the persistent sun tried to burn holes through the polluted clouds that hung overhead. Boy shifted his feet nervously and felt the crunching of broken glass beneath his thin shoes.

"And remember, when we reach the end of the alley, you go left and I go right. Keep your eyes closed the whole time or we will lose our connection. Follow your instincts. Trust me. With our energy, we will find each other."

Elle's repeated instructions did not inspire much more confidence in the concept. Purposely straying through the unfamiliar passageways of an unfriendly city did not seem the best way to prove that a friendship was forming. Boy would rather just have taken her word for it, but as he was learning quickly, Elle Lavender lived life by swinging from one whim to the next.

They closed their eyes together and took their first hesitant steps into the long, narrow alleyway. They walked with their hands outstretched against the cool brick walls until their fingers fell and felt nothing. Elle drifted right on her own way and Boy crept left, second guessing each blind step with an uneasy breath. The jarring sounds of machinery flooded in through the tunneled passages as Boy stumbled into dead ends and garbage cans, fumbling his way deeper into the maze. With each turn he became more and more disoriented, waiting for some sort of supernatural signal to guide him. As he worked his way ahead the walls closed in on him, forcing him to turn sideways and fight to slip through a gap. He stood in the opening with his arms spread and began to feel a gentle tingle in his fingertips. He fought the temptation to open his eyes, out of fear that he would break their connection. It felt as if a magnet was hovering in front of him, pulling him in, but after two or three hurried steps he tripped and fell.

Boy sat up stiffly holding his elbow and looked back to see that he had tripped over the legs of a homeless man lying in the alleyway next to a dumpster. The man was barefoot and covered in crusted dirt. He was wearing a white tee shirt with the image of a melted clock on the front and torn jeans covered in splatters of paint. The man had a damp cardboard box covering his head. The startled man appeared to have been sleeping because he flailed wildly at Boy's unexpected presence and the box slid off of his head. The man was old and withered with gnarled white hair. His face was creased like a statue and his frame was gaunt and starved, but his eyes were a beautiful palette of picturesque colors, nearly the same as the ones that were staring back at him, and they were swirling to a stop.

Boy scrambled away from the man until his back hit the brick of the alley wall behind him. The man blinked several times, focusing on

Boy's frightened face. He leaned his head from side to side, his neck cracking, and his split lips revealing rotting teeth beneath. An air conditioner steadily dripped fluids onto him from above and he grimaced at every drop. There was jaded disgust etched into the cracks around the man's frown.

"Lost?"

Boy refused to respond.

"Best way to find me I suppose," the man's voice was raspy and underwhelmed.

"Even if you had never come, here is where you would arrive. I know what you seek, but you are searching on the wrong side of your eyes."

The man took a long look at the sordid alleyway that surrounded him and spat on the ground beside him.

"You remind me of me. If I could peel back time and stare at myself I would see you, but what would you see if you flirted with the future? What would it reveal to you? Allow me to show you."

The man stuck out his hand and waited for Boy to take hold of it.

"Never accept what *is*, over what could be."

When he noted Boy's indecision, he became offended, and his outstretched hand began to tremble in the air.

"I'm going back with or without you."

Boy could feel the gravity behind the man's stare. He lifted his hand that was now covered in filth from the alley floor and placed it in the stranger's shaking grip.

Boy did not want to be left behind.

The man leaned back against the wall and closed his eyes.

Chapter 4: Mr. Man's Mansion

Boy could feel the invasive colors surging through his veins. They crawled up his arms, pumped through his neck and began to coat his eyes. The colors splattered and dripped across his vision until the world around him became blindingly white. He felt weightless, as if he were flying, but as the colors began to separate and the world around him took shape he realized he being swept to the face of a rushing waterfall. He tumbled and kicked and clawed at the water as he was thrown over the edge. The imaginary gravity dragged Boy down violently, spitting him out head first onto a polished glass floor. He slid to a squeaky stop in front of an immaculately shined dress shoe that tapped impatiently in front of his nose. The shoe belonged to the foot of a flawlessly groomed middle-aged man wearing a white pinstripe tuxedo. The man's hair was combed and gelled neatly to one side. His eyebrows were boxy and every tooth in his mouth was a perfect square. The man crossed his arms courteously behind his back and gave Boy a slight bow as he rose to his feet.

"Welcome to my mind."

Boy and the man were standing in the center of a pearl white lobby that had the reverberate air of an empty museum. The entirety of the man's mind was framed by one spacious room, hollow but with great depth. The room was composed of three grand walls and the waterfall that had rinsed Boy served as the fourth. The illusory walls were lined with stretched blank canvasses and empty portrait frames as if the art had yet to be imagined. In each corner sat a large chunk of unsculptured granite waiting for an idea to shape them. The ceiling was a thin crystal mirror reflecting back down onto the glass floor, creating an infinite loop of echoing images of Boy and the strange man. His mind had no hallways, doorways, or windows to the outside. There seemed to be only one way in and no way out.

"Do not fear. It would be a pleasure to be trapped in here," he said.

The man slid his fingernail into a gap between two of his perfectly square teeth, inspected the findings, and then rapidly flossed with his finger. He pulled his lips back with his fingers and studied his smile in his reflection before letting the skin of his mouth snap back into place. The man turned to Boy with an elevated chin, apparently satisfied with the audit of his aesthetic.

"Would you like a tour?" he offered.

Boy marveled at the man's fantasy that was so far-fetched from his own.

"Excellent, let us begin," he said, nodding approval to himself.

Boy looked expectantly around the room, waiting to be guided, but the man stood still and unbothered, so Boy shoved his hands in his pockets and waited.

"We will not be taking the tour," the man said, "The tour will be taking us."

Faint yet distinct sounds of the rainforest echoed above Boy's head. Beads of sweat rolled out of his pores as the air around him thickened and choked him with humidity. The surging waterfall began to glisten exotically green and from out behind the face of the fall, a winding, diamond-printed python with beady yellow eyes slithered towards them. A jungle of trees and plants tumbled down behind the serpent, and as the water flooded in, the room converted into a dense canopy. Lofty trees sprung and unfolded their branches like umbrellas, thatched, elaborately woven furniture scattered itself throughout the mansion and thick vines draped from the ceiling. The blank canvases that stretched across the walls had been water-painted with dramatic Amazonian panoramas and reptilian irises. The granite blocks had been carved away and sculpted into twisting, godly serpent statues that coiled above their domain.

When the water finally settled and drained, Boy's bones could feel the vibrations of the jungle that engulfed him. The slithering snake that crept through the grass approached Boy from behind, wrapping itself tightly around his leg. He reached down and tried to pry the snake off of him but the serpent lunged and sank his short fangs into his wrist. The man watched Boy struggle with fiendish delight before emitting a sharp hiss that instructed the snake to unwind itself.

"He isn't accustomed to the company of guests. He lacks etiquette I am afraid."

Boy's wrist throbbed and swelled. He pressed down between the two bite marks and a green slime oozed out of the puncture holes.

"It's only poisonous if you believe it to be," the man said as the snake slid through his legs and exited the room through the base of the waterfall.

"Shall we continue?"

The man's question froze in the air as a shocking chill passed through the room. Boy watched his breath harden to crystals, leaving frigid daggers hanging from his lips. The waterfall iced over mid-cascade and hungry roars echoed from behind the glacial wall. The ice began to crack and shatter as a starved polar bear, a monstrosity of a beast with fur drooping from his skeleton, lumbered into the arctic room. At once, the man's mansion transformed again. The jungle was replaced by an ice palace from the coldest depths of fantasy. Frozen furniture skated into position around the room; spiraling stalactites corkscrewed down to form a chandelier, and vivid portrayals of arctic hunts with bloodied fangs appeared in the frames on the walls. Ice sculptures of malicious wintry beasts displaced the serpent statues that loomed in the room's dark corners. A scorching log fire lit itself in the center of the room with a giant flash.

The glacial beast confronted Boy, standing on its rear legs and brandishing its razor sharp claws from its chafed paws. He tilted his head back and let out a vociferous roar that cracked the crystal ceiling, causing icy shards to rain down from above. Boy took a step backwards and the man in the tuxedo intervened coolly.

"No need to show off my friend," the man said soothingly, running his hand along the exposed spine of the bear, which growled and exited the room through the gap in the waterfall that he had created upon entering.

"And now, for my favorite room of the house," he smiled his square toothed smile and waved his hand at the congealed waterfall as it turned to liquid gold. A majestic black tiger with thick golden stripes stalked across the floor, dragging a broken metal chain from its neck. The ice thawed and melted jewels dripped from the crevices, coating the palace in opulence. The décor of the man's mansion put to shame the revered royal houses of the past, proving once more that there was no luxury that the mind could not afford.

Two tremendous thrones twisted into place, facing each other in the center of the room. The man obliged his guest to take a seat with a motion of his hand. The extravagant tiger laid by the man's feet with his tongue hanging out of his mouth.

The man in the white suit crossed one leg neatly over the other and patted his hair down meticulously. Boy observed him uncomfortably from the edge of his throne.

"A beautiful gift it is to be able to escape, isn't it? When you don't wish to be somewhere, you can be anywhere." The man clapped his hands together and shook them vigorously.

"You think this is unbelievable, but I believed it, and so it became. What did I want from the world? *Absolutely nothing.* All I wanted was my own, so I created it, and here we are."

The man's voice oozed with protected pride.

"Who am I? No one of much importance I'm afraid. You would not recognize my name if I told it to you and I could only tell it to you if I could remember it. They call you Boy? You may call me Man… Or rather, Mr. Man. It's important to show respect where it is due. You may not think you know me or that I know you, but we are one in the same. We are connected now. But enough about us, you want to know about me."

The man twisted his body sideways and dropped his head towards Boy.

"You see child, I have a distaste for reality. It is dull, suffocating, and there are far too many senseless rules. There are rules but yet there is no one in control. Where lies the logic? The universe embraces the chaos; it allows those to exist but does nothing more and nothing less. It claims it is not the cause but only the effect. No, when I was young and saw a world without a purpose it frightened me. I reverted inward. My mind became my home, as it is so often yours. I realized how vivid this world could be, how free, and have never cared to return. I spend my time in the 'real' world only to survive, but this is where I come to *live*."

Mr. Man pressed his middle finger firmly into his temple.

"It is a curse and a blessing my friend, embrace it but don't trust it. As you can see, you can share your mind with those who, well, need more space… but be careful with what they bring in with them. Heed my warning; the imagination is no place for that which is real. All that is real is alive, and all things that live must die. You can only trade pain for pain – there is no other way. You cannot have dreams without nightmares as you cannot understand light without the darkness. I speak cryptically because life is a horrible riddle whether you understand the joke at the end or not."

Mr. Man reached forward and grabbed Boy's wrist.

"What are you afraid of? What do you fear?"

Boy glanced down at the tiger looking up at him. The beast chewed on his metal chain with gold-dipped fangs. He stopped to stare at Boy and let the chain fall from his teeth. Boy wondered if all fear was only imagined, and if it was, would inside of an imagination be the only place to be afraid?

"You don't know? How do you not know? How do you not understand the workings of your own mind? One of your only friends I assume. Quite the pretentious relationship."

He scoffed.

"People told me my entire life that it was fear that kept me in here. I told them that it was freedom. There is no freedom out there. I told them of all of the places that I could create for them, an existence without limits. But they didn't believe in the world that I saw, so I created what they couldn't see." Mr. Man grinded his perfectly square teeth as he spoke.

"Ignorance was too bliss. Out there we are what we are, but in here, and in there –" he pointed to what lie behind Boy's eyes "– we can be anything. We can look however we want, do whatever we want, be whoever we want. We are gods amongst our own creations."

Mr. Man rose to his feet, kicking his throne over backwards and the floor swallowed it whole. The tiger let out a roar like a firing engine and dropped its head low to the ground. Mr. Man spun around and screamed at Boy, "This is freedom!"

Mr. Man threw his hands into the air and a murder of crows swooped in over the waterfall carrying shadows in their claws. The entire mansion disappeared, draped in black until there was only a single light left shining above a new painting that had appeared on the stretched canvas on the wall.

"What do you think?" Mr. Man asked, leading Boy with a hand on his shoulder towards the work of art.

Brushed onto the canvas was the portrayal of a terrified boy hanging from the edge of a cliff by a slipping hand. On top of the cliff was a pair of dead trees and cracked dry earth. The land was barren and wasted for as far as the eye could see. The painting cut off just beneath the boy's dangling legs so it could not be seen what was below him. A melting sun over the hanging boy's shoulder dripped amber droplets onto the floor below the painting. Boy watched a puddle of paint form at his feet.

"Are we drowning?" Mr. Man asked, looking down and staring at his image in the puddle.

"Will the ones above the surface save us? Or are we their reflections they refuse to see? Should we be saving them?"

The boy who had been hanging from the cliff in the painting could now be seen sinking into the depths of the melted sun's puddle.

"Perhaps it is a far better place that you fall to, than that which you hang on to."

Mr. Man stomped his foot into the puddle and the amber paint splashed onto the legs of his white tuxedo.

"Fear or freedom?" he asked, looking over his shoulder and staring into the lonely light shining down on them.

Boy saw a colorful tear trickle down Mr. Man's face and could feel one falling from his own eye. He caught the falling drop on the end of his finger and held it up to the spotlight.

"Or are they one in the same?"

Chapter 5: Flight of the Fireflies

The hungry thunder rumbled as Boy sat in front of his window with the curtain closed, his mind caught between the fringes of two worlds. Boy's encounter with Mr. Man in his mansion had affected him deeply. The warning was veiled in rhetoric but unmistakable in its message. The effort exerted by the boy in the painting to remain dangling from the cliff gave the impression that there was reason to resist, but he refused to look down, and therefore knew nothing of the consequence of the fall. Thus, he feared only the fall itself. Boy had watched that hand slipping, clawing at crumbling rock, over and over again trying to determine if the fear would ultimately be worse than the fall. Mr. Man wanted him to let go.

Boy struggled to shut off his thoughts, as they pulled him further and further inside of himself to the point that he felt he would disappear altogether. He had met a man who lived inside of his mind, a man who had forsaken the world around him in order to embellish the world within him, a man who had given up nothing in exchange for everything. It was a dangerously enticing concept; one that would be considered, as Boy's stagnant quest for heroism in reality contrasted sharply with his valiant success in his imagination and forced him to doubt where he truly belonged.

The bed beneath Boy creaked as Elle stood and glided across the dark room in her socks. She knelt down quietly in front of a small patch of singed wallpaper that clung to the charred wall. Her long fingers strolled through the garden of burnt flowers before beginning to peel at the flaking stems and petals. She scratched at the paper until her fingernails were black with aged ash and a speck of white wall shyly revealed itself.

Boy watched her curiously from beneath his blanket, with the dissonant thunder contributing to the mystery of her mannerisms. Elle's persona had proven to be amorphous. Her mood never correlated with the moment but she never second guessed her sentiments, always electing to feel exactly what she was feeling, not attempting to manipulate her emotions in any way. Elle's unpredictability made her irresistible to Boy's attention and when he wasn't wandering about his own worlds, he wanted nothing more than to be a part of hers. Boy believed that in some way Elle was an answer to a question that he struggled to form. Destiny didn't play dice, her presence was not random.

A crack of lightning interrupted the observational silence and Elle turned to the sound of nature as if it had called her name.

She found Boy's eyes in the dark and asked him, "Have you ever caught a firefly before?"

Boy deliberated, trying to remember times that he could not remember.

"That's such…a shame."

There was poison in Elle's voice. She turned back to the burnt wall and meditated. Boy wondered where her mind wandered in the silence.

"Let's go find one," she said after several mute minutes of rumination.

Elle rose to her feet, pulled off her socks, balled them up, and rolled them under her bed. She called Boy over with a bend of her index finger and then glided out of the room, leaving the door wide open behind her.

***

"It's not about where you look, it's about how you look," Elle whispered to Boy as they crept through the backyard.

Boy, who was staggering blindly trying not to trip over his own feet, wasn't sure how to apply this new search strategy. He settled on squinting his eyes and crouching slightly lower, but as obscure as it was he couldn't see anything. Elle, however, seemed to thrive in the elements. She examined the grass blade by blade, and then went in and out, up and over the bushes until she reached the only tree in the yard and climbed it. She hugged the trunk and stood on a gnarled branch to scan the small patch of land but there were no holes in the darkness. She sighed and jumped down from the tree and sat in the wet grass.

"We will let them come to us," she decided.

Boy sat down directly in front of her.

"How are you going to find the fireflies if you are looking at me?" she asked quietly.

Boy scooted himself by her side.

Elle tucked her arms into her lavender dress and rested her chin in the palms of her hands. The gentle rain turned into a steady rain and they both began to shiver. Boy inched himself closer to her so that their shoulders were touching.

"We will wait for them," Elle said.

"They know where we are. Even if we can't see them, they can see us."

And so they let the time pass, the rain fall, and their bones chill, waiting for a firefly to find them.

"Do you even know what we are looking for?" Elle asked.

Boy plucked a damp blade of grass from the ground.

"Fireflies, Boy, fireflies," Elle said in exasperation.

Elle looked up at the rain and watched the drops fall on her.

"I can't imagine never having caught a firefly. I think that's the only reason they exist, for us to catch them. I think they like when we chase them because we don't keep them, we just hold them and let them go."

Elle lashed out with her hand towards the sky as if she were trying to catch a lightning bolt in her palm. Perhaps she was, Boy thought.

"My mom used to tell me to catch all of the fireflies before they disappeared. She said that when you get older they all go away. I asked her where they go and she told me that nobody knows; that maybe they get captured by the streetlamps, the headlights, or the T.V.

screens. Everything that makes the city shine I guess, but I don't believe that."

Elle rocked herself back and forth and forth and back.

"I don't think that they go anywhere. I think that people just stop looking for them. That's why they never know where to find them."

Elle hung her head.

"It's been too long since I caught a firefly. I would give anything to know where they went."

Boy never knew they had existed and didn't know where they might have gone. He could imagine a place though, for her – a perfect home for the fireflies waiting to be chased. Boy could see it clearly, the phosphorescent fantasy, and he wanted to take Elle there. Boy looked down skeptically at the hand that had transported him to Mr. Man's mansion and placed it gently into Elle's open palm. Elle locked her fingers between his without taking her gaze off of the sky.

Boy squeezed his eyes shut and after a short breath his colors began to empty. He became lightheaded as they rushed down through his veins and surged into Elle. The colors pumped their way up her slender neck and melted across her irises. Her vision was coated with chromatic streaks until the world around her had been painted over.

Hand in hand, Boy and Elle fell back gently into the wet grass.

***

"I have your eyes."

Elle watched the colors swirl in her reflection in the puddle on the cracked street under her feet. Her borrowed irises wandered about the shadows of unimagined darkness. The misting rain dried in the sky and Elle pulled her hand away from Boy's slowly as if they were passing notes in class. She held back her burning questions, preferring to embrace the mystery of the moment as she approached a pair of bicycles leaned against a flickering lamp post. She wheeled out the bicycle with the purple frame, knowing exactly who it was for, and threw her leg over the seat. Boy mounted the bicycle with the white paint and rolled up beside her.

"So, where are we going?" Elle asked, raising her eyebrows and lifting her foot to the pedal.

Boy reached forward and tapped his finger on the lid of the Mason jar that sat in the middle of a metal basket in front of the handlebars. Inside of the clear jar there was a flash of light followed by a series of sparks that jumped from side to side. Within an instant, the fireflies inside of the jar were beaming and a melodic buzz hummed around them. Elle knocked her knuckles on the glass jar in her own basket to wake her fireflies, raising a cyclone of sparkles that served as her headlight.

Above the two riders there was one strobing beacon of light that was free from their jars. It darted back and forth, streaking the night sky to capture their attention, and then flew over their heads away from the dimly lit street and spliced through the darkness. Elle and Boy swung their bicycles around and pedaled after the fleeting flash of light, seeing no more than a few feet in front of them.

The ink-black road led them through a sleeping neighborhood tucked in by shadows. Boy's spinning tires screeched to a stop and Elle slammed on her brakes beside him. Elle squinted at the peculiar silhouettes that surrounded them and Boy watched their guiding firefly float to the ceiling of the sky. All at once, a swarm of jumping lights rose from the edges of the neighborhood, skipping through the thin air like a storm of shooting stars. Within seconds, a sea of light flooded the streets like a stadium. From the shadows emerged two rows of the most rare and unusual houses that the mind could construct. The architecture defied laws and limits – each home a homage to the mental modern arts. There was every type of house imaginable: a stilted house made of glass, a house built into trees, a house built upside down with a basement for a roof. There was an aquarium house, a flat house, a hovering house, a house made of seashells, and even an edible, candy-coated house. Each house in the neighborhood was absolutely unique, and Elle walked beside her bicycle, stopping and staring at every single one. Her eyes turned from the homes up to the sky of fireflies lighting their street.

"This is the New Road, the way it should have been. Is this where the fireflies live?" Elle asked.

Boy shook his head and swung himself back onto his bicycle. The sky above them shifted forward as the swarm of fireflies began their journey home. Elle and Boy pedaled frantically after them, chasing the flashing lights to the end of the neighborhood where a long, winding driveway awaited them. The fireflies funneled themselves between the trees that bordered the pavement and led the riders into a clearing that revealed a dormant city resting beneath them.

The lethargic metropolis gave off an abandoned air, a ghostly hush that lacked peace in its stillness. Two slender skyscrapers full of silhouette people stabbed through the gloomy clouds at their sides. The population within the high-rises was paralyzed by the flashing screens in front of them. A cacophony of recorded sounds served as a somber soundtrack to the vacant city. A distant blare of horns honking came from a line of rusted cars hitched together, circling the two towers like a toy train around a Christmas tree.

At their side, flapping its wings like a tired bird was a mammoth airplane, shuttling its hypnotized passengers through the bleak sky. Elle and Boy came to a stop next to the firefly and as they watched the human outlines pass by, staring straight ahead, their faces glowing, their eyes unblinking, not a single soul looked back at them through their window.

As Elle lamented the view of the somber city, the mass of fireflies that lit the night were disappearing into the obscurity ahead of them. The final stretch of driveway sloped like a ramp and by the light of the fireflies she could finally see the place that she could never imagine.

Elle revved her handlebars with two twists of her wrists and took one last look over the edge at the world that she was so familiar with and felt sorry for it. She wished there was a bicycle for every one of them. She wished that they knew how close they were to the land of the fireflies. She wished they were looking for them.

Elle lifted her lace-less sneaker and gave a kick that sent the pedals spinning and sent her racing down the ramp. As her wheels spun wildly she was reminded of a feeling that once was easy to find, but lately was nowhere to be found. It was a reminiscent rush – so simple, yet so sacred. She pushed her churning legs to their limits, balancing her fear of falling with her fascination of flying atop those two swirling wheels.

She squeezed her breaks and slid to a stop next to Boy's parked bike at the foot of a dirt trail. They removed their glass jars of fireflies from their baskets and walked over to a rickety wooden fence that ended their path. In the middle of the fence there was a latched gate that served as the entrance. Elle turned to Boy and tapped her jar against his to make a silent toast. The clouds of fireflies above them sailed over the fence posts and returned to their home, leaving Elle and

Boy with just the glowing light from their jars. Elle placed her hand on the door's latch and then paused, "We should knock. We are guests."

Elle tapped her knuckles against the wood and the latch lifted and the gate swung open. Elle's face burned with brilliant light as if she was kissing the sun. She did not blink or shield her eyes, but lifted a finger into the air.

"It is a luminescent place,
Where translucent children play
Games with no purpose,
Speaking languages that are wordless
In open fields of freedom.

Lucid humans lit by stars to be held,
Where the hands of the clock hold nothing,
Where there is never more than now,
Where time is never lost,
It is only ever to be found.

Where life stands still
And only the fire flies,
Where the dreamers chase the dream
Across their infinite lives."

Elle lowered her finger and turned her glowing face to Boy.

"They are exactly where I hoped they would be."

Elle dropped to one knee in the dirt and unscrewed the lid of the jar to free the final fireflies. They danced in the open air, hovering in front of Elle's lips, teasing her playfully.

"They want us to try and catch them," Elle said to Boy, who was releasing his own from his jar.

"That's why we are here isn't it?"

Elle winked at Boy and ran after the fleeing fireflies. Boy followed her to the other side of the fence, glancing briefly over his shoulder at the darkness behind them, and closed the gate gently.

There they would stay, chasing each other through the land of the fireflies, hoping that they could catch one another – even if just to let each other go again.

Chapter 6: In Living Color

The final tears dripped off of Elle's curled eyelashes before she twisted her fingers around the metal chain and drained the bathtub. She sat and watched the swirling water run away from her and said a silent goodbye. Boy sat on the floor with his back against the toilet, balancing a pen on the back of his knuckles while staring blankly at the empty lines in front of him.

Elle's presence had inspired Boy to write in his journal and add to his struggling story. She was more than a muse: she was the catalyst of the action, she was a main character, but she wasn't the conclusion he was desperate for. From the day they met Boy had hopes that he could be her hero and that she would be that one person whose salvation would validate his heroism, but it had become apparent that Elle Lavender did not need saving.

"I know you are writing about me in there," Elle said, standing on the edge of the tub.

Boy folded the corner of the page disappointedly and shoved the journal into his waistband.

"I know how hard it must be trying to capture my essence. It isn't easy describing originality. What is there to compare me to?" Elle said with a big smile, retying the shoelace that held up her hair.

"The dress is very important. Some would say it is pivotal to my character."

Elle washed her hands in the sink and splashed water on her face as she spoke.

"I don't want to read it, whatever it is, not even the first page. Well, maybe the first page but definitely not the second."

Elle shook her hands dry and elbowed down the light switch as Boy stood and followed her into the hall.

"And don't forget to mention my suitcase. You might as well be writing about someone else if you don't mention the suitcase."

Elle and Boy had developed a routine of escapism, drifting away into Boy's fantasies and then crashing back down to reality on the sordid bathroom floor. Boy meticulously crafted worlds to fit the design of Elle's oddities. They were psychedelic and surreal without rules or rationality, and there they flourished. But pretend perfection was only so therapeutic, and Elle, not one to avoid her afflictions, understood that the escape was temporary and that their problems persisted. Boy would have lived in his mind with Elle forever had she wanted the same.

They never actually acknowledged their imagined escapades. It felt like a secret even amongst themselves. It was impossible to explain, but they owed an explanation to no one. Boy worried that one day someone would realize the gift that he had been given and come to take it away from him. They did not include Leo in their fictitious existence, for they knew he was not a proponent of the make believe. They were unsure of how he would process such a blatant contradiction to the rules of reality and were worried that he would not be able to cope with the anomaly. Thus they opted to shelter him, locking the bathroom door behind them as they ascended into the realms of fantasy. Leo never even knew how far away his friends were because he too was immersed in other worlds, worlds of words written by historic hands, hoping that those hands would one day write about him.

Leo closed his book and tossed it on his pillow as he joined Elle and Boy in the middle of the bedroom. Elle unzipped her suitcase and handed out juice boxes around their circular triangle.

"How long have these been in there?" Leo asked skeptically, as he struggled to stab the plastic straw through the hole of the carton.

"Truthfully, I don't remember ever putting them in there," Elle said blankly.

"They are still cold," Leo said with surprise after taking a sip.

"How is that even possible?"

"I have no idea, but if you want another one let me know. I have about nine and a half full ones in there."

Elle flattened her already empty juice box with her hands and chewed on the straw.

"Mathematically it doesn't make sense that you could have a half of something that is full," Leo pointed out.

"Did it make mathematical sense when you used three pieces of bread to make a sandwich?" Elle asked.

"It was a matter of ratio between peanut butter and jelly, so actually yes it did make mathematical sense," Leo clarified.

"If you are upset you can insult me," Elle offered.

"You just took the fun out of it," Leo said, sipping his juice box.

Elle let out a prolonged sigh of boredom that spoke for everyone in the room. The summer would start and end without anyone realizing the season had cycled. There was not much to talk about and even less to do, but Elle always found a way to pass the time somewhere deep within her bottomless suitcase.

She leaned over and searched through her luggage, nearly the entire top half of her body disappearing within the stretched canvas, and pulled out a thick stack of used magazines. She shuffled through them, tossing the ones she had already read to the side.

"I used to steal a magazine every time I went to the dentist's office," Elle said.

"You must have had some really bad teeth," Leo commented as he watched the pile of discarded magazines stack up.

"No, I never even had braces. I would just go to the dentist's office to steal their magazines. I didn't even need an appointment," she said.

Elle flung a magazine like a Frisbee onto Leo's lap. "Here is one for you. It looks like it has a planet on the cover or something. I know you like space."

"This is the Earth," Leo said, pointing to the cover with his finger.

"How would I know, I've never had a chance to take a good look at it." Elle fluttered her eyelashes.

"And for you," she directed at Boy, "Art in early 20th century France, because, well, I don't want to read it," she admitted, and flicked it at him like a dirty tissue.

Elle held up a magazine with a tropical island on the cover.

"*Dream Destinations*, what a coincidental title, I was just dreaming about being somewhere else," she said, flipping through the pages with a false sense of interest.

"Oh look, they offer dolphin cruises with breakfast on board in Hawaii. How accommodating of them," Elle muttered.

"I went whale watching once and I got really sick," Leo commented.

"Yeah, I'm not surprised, whales are disgusting," Elle responded without looking up from her magazine.

"What?"

"What?"

In the midst of confusion, the bedroom door flung open and Miss Jennie stepped into the room wearing a faded watermelon colored dress.

"What are you doing?"

No one looked up from their magazine.

"I distrust…*this*," she motioned vaguely to their strangely shaped seating arrangement.

"We need to talk," she said forcefully after being ignored.

"Me?" Leo asked.

"Never in your life," said Miss Jennie.

"Boy?"

"Who?"

"Him."

"Obviously not."

Elle stood and flattened her dress and silently stepped into the hall with Miss Jennie behind her.

"I can't wait to go to space," Leo said over the top of his magazine once the door had closed.

"I don't want to go without my dad, though. He is the one who taught me everything I know about space. I don't think I would appreciate it without him. It wouldn't be the same."

Although he spoke casually, Boy could see that Leo's fingernails were digging into the glossy paper.

"I don't think I've ever said this out loud," he said, now rolling the magazine in his hands, "but it was never really my dream, it was my dad's dream to be an astronaut. He is the one who used to talk about it all of the time. I think he gave me away so he could focus on trying to make it to space, but I just don't understand why he had to give me up; I told him that I wanted to go with him."

Boy avoided Leo's searching eyes and stared down at his burnt shoes.

"I don't know if he ever made it to outer space. Part of me hopes he didn't so that we can go together for the first time, and part of me hopes that he did so he will be ready to have a family again. When he is ready to have a family, I know he will come for me. He knows where I am; he is the one who left me here."

Leo tossed the magazine onto the floor.

"If he doesn't come back for me I think I am going to go to him. Elle was right, what are we really waiting for? It wouldn't just be running away because I know where I would be going. Well, I don't know exactly where he would be but I have an idea. I've been doing some research, but then again, I just don't want to be out looking for him if he comes looking for me, you know?"

The door swung open and Elle stepped back into the bedroom with her hands clasped, spinning one thumb over the other.

"What did she want?" Leo asked.

"Fashion advice," she lied.

"Are you in trouble?" Leo asked.

"Me? For what? I didn't pick out that dress."

"Do you ever take anything seriously?"

"I take what is serious, seriously."

"Is it something bad?"

"Bad," Elle snorted at the word, "My grandma used to tell me to kiss the small bad before it becomes a big bad. If you tell yourself that everything is beautiful you will never know how to look ugly in the eyes when it is talking to you. Bad isn't as scary as it sounds."

Elle slowed the spinning of her thumbs and conceded, "Miss Jennie had news for me, that's all."

"Good news?" Leo asked.

"That depends on what news you are hoping for."

Elle looked at her wrist as if she were wearing a watch.

"What will be the date one week from today?"

Leo's brain served as her calendar.

"The thirteenth," he said.

"That is unlucky," Elle said with a shudder.

"What will happen in a week?"

Elle promptly ended the interrogation with the wave of her hand and turned her focus to the small patch of white wall that she had freed with her fingernail the night she chased fireflies.

"I am going to paint this," she said, heading directly to her suitcase, which no one doubted had the supplies inside.

She pulled out a small brush and a tray for the paints and sat down in front of the patch. Elle mixed the colors and hummed to herself quietly. Boy walked over to the wall and watched her work. Without looking behind her, Elle raised the brush over her head and handed it to him. She grabbed the corner of his tee shirt and pulled him closer to the wall.

"Paint me a portrait, Boy," Elle said, laying down and posing on her side.

"I want it to look like my twin," she said, winking at Boy artfully.

Boy held the brush clumsily in his fingers and his hesitant hand floated in front of the wall. Elle let him struggle briefly before grabbing his wrist and guiding it.

"It's just like that, nothing more nothing less."

Elle put her finger on a light blue stain on the collar of Boy's white shirt and shook her head.

"Already making a mess," she said, but did a double take when she noticed the red paint on the end of the brush.

"Strange," she commented, tracing back from the stain up to Boy's fidgeting eyes.

Elle snatched the brush out of his hand and pointed it in his face threateningly, "If we are going to best friends, you need to talk."

Boy said nothing.

"Just say anything."

Boy didn't say anything.

"Ask me a question, or just make a noise, your silence is unacceptable. I feel like you would have so much to say if you would just let yourself say it," Elle said.

Boy considered his options. He had a question he wanted to ask her since the very first day they met, but he didn't know how to ask it without just asking it.

Boy picked up the tray of paints and pointed at each color, one after another, and then extended it out to Elle.

"I don't get it," Elle said.

Boy did the exact same thing again except slower.

"I still don't get it," Elle said again except slower.

This time, Boy picked up the brush and dipped it in the puddle of yellow paint, then drew a thin line on the wall. He wiped off the end of the brush and dipped it in the green and drew another line next to the first. Once he had streaked the wall with every color in the tray he drew a small curving question mark beneath the stripes and handed the brush back to Elle.

She looked at the wall, looked at Boy, looked back at the wall, and then to Boy again.

"What is my favorite color?"

Boy nodded.

Elle stuck the paintbrush behind her ear and cracked her knuckles with a grin.

"My favorite color is purple, which you probably could have guessed because my last name is Lavender. Even if it wasn't I would still pick purple because it is such a potent color, you know? It says a lot with so little, it is dramatic, fierce but yet calm. It is the most mysterious color that you can interact with. To be clear, I love all colors – they are all unique and necessary. I wouldn't even want to imagine a world without colors. You wouldn't be able to tell anything apart, you wouldn't be able to express yourself and everything would be so unoriginal. What could be worse than that?"

Elle's words were shooting rapid fire and Boy was embracing every bullet.

"Believe it or not, this reminds me of a poem." Elle's pointer finger shot up into the air.

Leo put down the book that he had picked back up and turned his attention to Elle, the self-proclaimed aspiring poet.

"The girl who wrote the poem was in a car crash that killed her parents and made her blind – physically blind, as opposed to metaphorically blind, which is basically the whole point of the poem. She could still see but she couldn't make out shapes, all she saw was floating blobs of color. I can't remember the whole thing but the first few lines are special."

Elle stood and held her hands together in front of her as if she were reciting a prayer.

"It goes:

'From the darkness I lived in color

I did not hide,

I dug my toes in sands of melted crayons

I did not hide,

I swam in rainbow rivers and climbed trees with confetti leaves

I did not hide,

I grew in the shade of shadow

I did not hide,

I wandered as kaleidoscopes guided my eyes

I did not hide,

My life was a painting unfrozen in time

I did not hide,

I was not hidden.

I saw everything.

I have seen everything.'"

Elle slowly lowered herself down onto her knees next to Boy.

"It goes something like that."

After a moment of reflection Leo called out from his race car bed in the corner of the room, "Is it still a poem if the whole thing doesn't rhyme?"

"It doesn't have to rhyme," Elle answered.

"Then what makes it a poem?" Leo asked.

"It's a poem because it is beautiful," Elle said.

Leo sucked his teeth.

"I beg to differ."

"Go ahead, beg."

Leo turned his attention safely back to his book.

Elle pulled out the brush from behind her ear and traced imaginary curves into the air in front of her. She held her elbow steady and loosened her wrist with small circles. She then dipped the brush into the black paint. "Come here," she instructed Boy.

Elle leaned forward and began to paint small uneven letters across the front of his shirt.

"*boy*", she read aloud.

"It's a nametag, so people can know who you are without you having to introduce yourself."

Elle leaned back to admire her work. "Don't wash it off."

Boy shook his head. He would never.

"Boy should be capitalized," Leo once again interjected from across the room.

"What do you mean?" Elle asked.

"You are saying that Boy is his name, so it needs to be uppercase."

"Maybe you have a point," she conceded, "but then again maybe you don't. I want you to think about that."

The bedroom door swung open once more and Miss Jennie stepped in looking flustered.

"I have to step out. Don't…do anything."

She shuffled a stack of documents that were slipping out of her arms.

"If you so much as breathe disrespectfully when I am gone I will make it harder for you to breathe at all when I return," she said, her eyes locked on Leo, and then slammed the door.

"She is the worst person on Earth," Leo said.

"That is such an interesting thought," Elle pondered out loud for everybody, "that out of all the people in the whole world, someone might actually be the worst and not even know it."

"Miss Jennie is the worst and she knows it," Leo said.

"That's a pretty big statement," Elle said.

"Do you remember that time she forced you to drink a smoothie that had every ingredient in the kitchen because you left the fridge door open?" Leo asked.

"My stomach still hurts."

"Exactly."

Leo threw his hands up in the air as his point was made.

"Wait, you aren't going to give more examples? I feel attacked," Elle protested.

She fired a finger at Boy, "You told me that she made Boy sleep in a garbage bag for a week because he wet the bed," Elle said.

Boy shot Leo a look.

"A long time ago, *so* long ago. My point is that she is a low quality human being."

Elle sighed.

"That is a very strong thing to say about someone that you barely know."

"We have lived here for ten years; we know everything that we need to know."

"What do you know about her then?"

"Enough."

"That is lazy and wrong. You don't know why she is the way she is and you have never tried to find a reason."

"There is no excuse for the way she is."

"I didn't say excuse. I said a reason."

In one swift motion Elle was on her feet and drifting into the hallway.

"Where are you going?" Leo called out.

"To investigate," Elle called back.

"But where?"

Elle wrapped her head through the doorway, "Where would you look for clues?"

"We can't go in there," Leo said as they stood anxiously in front of Miss Jennie's bedroom door.

"Yes we can. We shouldn't, but we can."

Elle dismissed the maze of locks that bordered the door and twisted the knob below with ease. She began to push open the door and then hesitated.

"Have you guys ever been in there?" Elle asked, her confidence wavering slightly.

The two boys shook their head in unison.

"Let's not be so dramatic," Elle said with a wiggle of her fingers.

She eased open the door and they stepped into the uncharted territory with caution. Miss Jennie's private life was far more unsettling than they had anticipated and they had expected the worst. It was as if a scrapbook had vomited across the walls, splattering faded newspaper clippings, torn photographs, and crumpled ticket stubs throughout every inch of the room. The décor was laid out as if Miss Jennie slept in the midst of a crime scene or she was trying to solve a complicated web of crimes herself and was struggling to find connections between the pieces of evidence.

In the center of her room there was a large recliner chair with worn armrests. It sat facing a small projector screen that was looping silent, grainy home videos. A happy pair of identical faces stared up at the shaky camera with guilty smiles. The two young girls on the screen were taped together from head to toe, with the clear adhesive mangling their lips and noses. They fought to pull apart from each other but only managed to wobble from side to side like bowling pins. As the two girls shook with laughter a hand reached in from out of the frame and began to unwind them. The sisters spun until they were completely unraveled, and then dizzily staggered into each other as they massaged their faces with their tiny hands.

The projector cut to the next clip which showed the two girls standing in their diapers passing a small kitten back and forth. One of the girls hoisted the miniature cat into the air and placed it on her sister's head like a helmet. Both the child and the panicked pet flailed and scratched at the other. As the camera wielding parent went to rescue the crying child, her sister fell onto her padded butt in a hysterical fit of giggles. The movie cut once more and the two sisters were now wading in not much more than a puddle of water that filled a small, inflatable pool in a driveway. They were wearing matching polka-dotted bathing suits and puffy orange floaties. The sisters held their arms out straight and swung them at each other, knocking each other in the mouths with their plastic-wrapped bubbles of air until they both fell over.

As Boy and Leo were mesmerized by the highlights of Miss Jennie's early life, Elle was scavenging the room for evidence. She could not defend the person who Miss Jennie had become, but Elle hoped to find shreds of innocence preserved somewhere in her past. Elle Lavender wanted to get to the source of Miss Jennie's suffering, and she knew the answer lie within those walls. But if those walls had spoken they would not have told a somber tale; there was nothing but happiness captured in the guarded memories. It was as close to a perfect life as could be portrayed, but somewhere along the line such an envious beginning took an ill-fated turn. Elle realized that it wasn't what she was seeing on the walls that would share Miss Jennie's secret but what was missing from them.

Next to Miss Jennie's bed there was one photograph that stood out from the rest. It was hung crookedly and there were wrinkles in the gloss from having been crumpled several times before. The photograph showed the two girls as early teenagers holding up a trophy together. Neither of them was smiling, nor looking directly at the camera. There was no photo hung next to it, just an empty white space like the one Elle had been painting in their room. Elle had a feeling that this was one of the last photos the two girls took together, and it was obviously not a happy memory.

Elle's eyes traced the wall from its blank space down to where it met the floorboards. In the crack between the wall and Miss Jennie's bed, she could see a crumpled ball of newspaper collecting dust. She pulled out the bedframe just enough to slide her arm into the gap and fish with her fingers for a corner of the paper. She reeled in the newspaper with a grunt and unraveled it carefully, revealing a black and white photograph diced by countless fold marks. The ink picture showed the mangled remains of a bicycle sprawled out on a sidewalk next to a school bus. Elle read the headline of the paper with a flooding sense of guilt. She then quickly crumpled the paper back into a ball and dropped it through the opening.

Elle pushed the bed against the wall with her thighs and turned her attention back to the picture of the girls holding the trophy. She lifted the photo from its bottom edge to allow herself a closer look when she saw a short message inscribed with a black marker on the back. She cautiously peeled the photo off of the wall and read what had been written. Elle struggled to hold the heavy photo steady in her trembling fingers. She understood why Miss Jennie could be the way that she was, but could not comprehend why the world could be the way that it was.

Elle taped the photo back to the wall with care, smoothing down the edges firmly so that it would never fall. Elle tapped both of the boys silently on the shoulder and herded them out of the room. Just as they exited, the front door crashed open and Miss Jennie's angry energy flowed down the skinny hallway. She was mumbling to herself about some injustice that the world had unrightfully spited her with. Boy closed her door silently behind them and they inconspicuously made their way back into their room.

The group stood together in the center of the carpet with their heads down, contemplating and processing all that they had seen. They weren't sure how to feel, nor knew what would ultimately change. They were left with more questions now than answers. They grappled with their conflicting sentiments and struggled to put the profound into words. The air around them was heavy with unaddressed pain.

"Life loves no one," Elle said finally, and one by one they climbed up the ladder to watch out of the window.

Chapter 7: Wasted Wishes

"What do you think they talk about?"

"Normal people things."

"Like what?"

"The weather."

"They can't always be talking about the weather," Leo said.

"There are lots of different types of weather," Elle said.

"But there is only one type of weather at a time," Leo said.

"Depends on where you are, the weather is different everywhere."

"True, but why would they be talking about other people's weather?"

"Everybody knows somebody with different weather," Elle said vaguely.

"I guess they could be talking about tomorrow's weather," Leo said.

"Or yesterday's weather."

"That's a good point."

"Or next week's weather."

"If they are trying to plan something outside," Leo added.

"That's exactly why," Elle confirmed.

"And so they know what to wear," Leo said.

"That is another good reason to talk about the weather," Elle said.

"It's important to talk about the weather," Leo said.

"People love talking about the weather," Elle said.

"Why do people love talking about the weather?"

"Because it's easy to talk about," Elle said.

"That's true."

"People will talk about the weather forever."

"What else do people talk about?"

"The stock market," Elle shrugged.

"Of course," Leo said, adjusting his glasses.

The three window watchers sat shoulder to shoulder to shoulder on Boy's bed, observing the family dinner taking place across the street, imagining what normalcy would sound like. Watching life from their crooked window was about as close as they could get to actually living it. They desperately dreamed of change, as guaranteed misery grew scarier than hypothetical unknowns, but soon they would learn a lesson that life so often teaches: that one must be very careful what they wish for.

"They look really happy," Leo said.

"It's easy to look happy, it's harder to be happy," Elle said passively.

"You don't think they are happy?" Leo asked.

"I hope they are," Elle said.

"I hope they are too," Leo said.

"It must be a special night," Elle commented.

"Why do you say that?" Leo asked, adjusting his head to get a better angle.

"She is wearing a new dress and she has her nails done. What is the date today?" She asked, interrupting her own observation.

"The twelfth," Leo said, eying Elle oddly.

"Hmm."

Elle put her finger on the window and pointed to the strawberry haired daughter who was bringing her dirty dishes to the sink. Elle looked at her own chipped nail against the glass and sat on her hands. A teenage boy with long wavy hair wearing a tight white tee shirt tucked into blue jeans joined the family at the table. The window watchers grunted their disapproval.

"The boyfriend is no good," Elle said.

"You can tell she loves him though," Leo guessed.

"She wants to love him," Elle corrected.

"What is stopping her?"

"His reckless love for himself."

Boy looked back and forth between the two, trying to see what they were seeing. He felt like he was missing something, or rather, everything.

"Wow, that's deep. How do you know all this stuff?" Leo asked.

"I am a girl. We know everything," Elle explained.

The three nodded in unison.

The girl's mother dimmed the kitchen lights and carried over a large chocolate cake covered in candles. The smiling daughter closed her eyes and took a deep breath; she clasped her hands together and blew out the candles. Her parents hugged her around the neck and clapped their happy hands while the boyfriend leaned back in his chair coolly and disinterestedly. The girl stood to pose for a photo in front of her cake, straightening her dress and tossing her hair over her shoulder.

A moment before the flash went off her ever-wandering eyes jumped to the window of 84 D, but Elle had already slid the raggedy curtain shut and sighed for the group.

"Happy birthday."

"I can't even remember the last time I had a birthday," Leo said sullenly.

"I am going to guess last year," Elle said.

"I mean celebrated a birthday, I know how old I am."

"I don't care how many birthdays I have. I'm never going to get old."

Elle tried not to think of her worn dress or the peeling soles of her sneakers which served as proof that time was passing.

"My question is, when was the last time that you made a wish?"

Elle looked to Boy who turned to Leo.

"Every single day," Leo said.

"No, a real wish, a wish that counts, a wish that you blow into the universe," Elle said.

"I am going to guess never," Leo said with cheerless sarcasm.

"Well, then it is never too late for a first time."

Elle climbed over the boys' legs, jumped to the ground and began to rummage through her suitcase. When she climbed back up the ladder her hands were full with a box of matches, a striped wax candle, and a plastic-wrapped cupcake.

"Hold these please," she handed off the matches to Boy and said to Leo, "Not you, for safety reasons," giving a nod to the burn scars on the wall. She unwrapped the cupcake, shoved the candle into the top with debatably excessive force, and held the match to the side of its box.

"Birthday rules are simple; you make a wish, pass the little cake, and the last wisher blows out the candle."

Elle struck the match and a flame grew from the air, but then she quickly waved it out of existence to add one more rule.

"Whatever you do, don't eat the cupcake at the end."

"You don't remember how long it's been in there?" Leo asked.

"I know *exactly* how long it's been in there," she said.

Elle lit a new match and held it to the candle's wick until it was infected by the fire.

"Ladies first," she said, closing her eyes to form her wish.

The boys watched patiently and considered their own desires carefully. When Elle had finished her turn she pulled open her eyes lazily and passed the cupcake across to Leo. She rested her head tenderly on Boy's shoulder and he held himself as still as could be.

Leo held the cupcake in his hands with conviction. He already knew his wish. He was basically born with it, and he didn't delay in professing it. He nodded his head to signal that his wish had been made and offered the cupcake to Boy who hesitated to receive it.

How would a boy who never had anything know what to ask for besides everything at once?

Elle raised her lips to Boy's ear.

"Make it a good one, Boy; we can't afford to waste a wish."

Boy was no stranger to that truth, and the longer that he stared into the wavering flame, the harder he begged the universe to give him a wish to wish. What it gave him instead was a vision. The flame was telling him a story and it was starting from the very beginning:

A small boy with his arms spread like wings running circles in a backyard with a white fence. A glove too big for his hand and a ball he was told to keep his eyes on. Little legs kicking through piles of raked leaves. Family photos held on the fridge by colored magnets. Pajama feet creeping down polished wooden stairs to steal a peek at presents under the tree. A rusty car doing laps around an empty parking lot. Young hands being held on a first date. Old hands clapping as their child crosses the stage. A boy moving out, a man moving in. A man is moved by the sight of a woman in all white walking towards him. The man watches a small boy with wide arms running circles in a backyard with a white fence. The man throws a ball to a hand in a glove that's too big. The man rakes leaves as high as the tree. The man hangs photos on the fridge with colored magnets.

The circle of life spun in the candle smoke before Boy's eyes. The fantasies of normalcy taunted him. Boy feared that if he were to succumb to the lure of the ordinary, he would fail in his quest to be extraordinary - to be a hero. If he were to wish for normality he would be forsaking his prophecy. The life inside of the fire was enticing, but it was one that he could not allow himself to wish for. The faces Boy had once seen in the burning wall fire returned to his flame. This time he could see them clearly. They were both very familiar to him, but the flame did not explain why they were burning together.

The candle in front of him was reaching the end of its wick. The wax melted, waiting for the wish from the wish-less boy. Boy let the flame go out. He refused to waste a wish.

Elle's voice broke the silence, "Thank you for revolving around the sun with me."

She hugged Boy and then Leo, who then hugged Boy loosely with one arm.

Although the air was heavy with weighted wishes, Leo appeared to have been reborn after their impromptu birthday party. His voice bounced with excited energy.

"I was so nervous when I was making my wish," Leo said as he slid down the bunk bed ladder.

"I was worried about how to word it because if you aren't careful you can curse yourself or something." Leo's hands jumped around his face as he spoke, not realizing the terrible irony he was headed for.

Elle saw where he was going and tried to stop him.

"Leo, please shut up," she begged, but Leo could not slow his tongue.

"I just wished that one day my dad and I would travel to space together, which you could have guessed, but I didn't say when because I don't want to rush…what happened?"

Elle's face had gone white and her eyes were wide in horror.

"Why are you looking at me like that?"

"Leo..." she struggled to begin, looking at Boy for confirmation, who refused to look at either of them.

"If you say your wish out loud it's never going to come true..."

"Why?"

"That's just how wishes work," Elle said.

Leo squeezed his eyes shut and pinched the bridge of his nose.

"Why didn't you tell me?"

"I thought you knew."

"You don't understand, this has to come true. It's the only dream I have."

Leo looked back and forth between Elle and Boy as if they had betrayed him, as if they and the universe were conspiring against him. Leo nodded his head up and down slowly in unpleasant agreement, but his words rejected the idea.

"I will find my father and we will be together." Leo spoke in fragmented chunks of words that he forced to have meaning.

He retrieved the box that he kept guarded in the corner of the room beside his bed. He held the box in an outstretched arm and showed it to Elle and then to Boy. He shook the box from side to side as if he were guessing the contents of a wrapped gift, then flipped it open and dumped it out onto the ground. Elle and Boy could only watch as his most precious possessions lost their sentiment before their eyes.

Leo stomped his foot on top of the pile of memories.

"If I can't find him then I can't go to space with him, and if I can't go with him he will go with someone else."

Leo stomped again, his face chillingly lacking expression. It was a mechanical meltdown.

"I used to hate this book," Leo said, picking up a small hardcover book that was leaning against his foot.

"Then I loved it, and now I hate it again. It makes no difference at all how I feel about it because the words never change."

Leo bounced the book back and forth in his hands, pulling at the cover and stressing the binding.

"It doesn't matter what I feel because nothing ever changes."

Leo took a small step and flung the book towards the crooked window. Elle and Boy ducked out of the way as it ripped through the curtain and shattered the thin glass of the window. Boy watched it fall to the sidewalk and land next to the feet of his strawberry blonde haired neighbor, who was sneaking into a black car that sat idling on their side of the street. The girl froze in place with her hand on the car door as the shards of glass rained down beside her. The girl's eyes jumped up to the shattered window and saw Boy looking down at her. The horn of the car honked lightly and she ducked into the passenger seat. The car sped off, crunching small pieces of broken glass beneath its tires.

What a time for a first impression, Boy thought to himself.

"Give me the candle," Leo demanded, his palm outstretched stiffly towards Elle.

"Give me the candle and I will wish it again."

Leo snatched the candle from the top of the cupcake and fumbled with the box of matches. He struck wildly at the side of the box, snapping the matches in two. One of the red tips eventually sparked into a small, shaking flame, but the candle had no wick left to burn. Leo let the lit match fall from his hand to the carpet and watched the small stick of fire smolder with vacant eyes.

"Leo," Elle called nervously as the carpet fibers began to smoke.

Leo turned his blank eyes up to Elle, who was perched to jump down from the bed, and gave her a big fake smile. He stomped his foot on the flame and dug the heel of his shoe into the carpet.

"Just a bad joke," he said, bending down and putting the box of matches inside of his now empty box of mementos. "I've never really been that funny."

Leo dragged his feet across the room and exited, closing the door all too gently behind him. For his friends it was not hard for them to understand his fragility, knowing that he was already broken. What more could they do but to allow him to shatter and wait to pick up the pieces?

"He's not okay Boy, we can't leave him alone right now," Elle said, backing down the bunk bed ladder. "I should have never told him to make that wish and I should have never told him that it wouldn't come true. He is too fragile…Boy!"

Boy's colorful eyes had begun to swirl as he created a safer space inside of his fantasy.

"No, no, no," Elle said, climbing back up the ladder. She propped herself up on the railing of the bed and delivered a swift slap across Boy's stoic face. His twisting eyes instantly came to a stop and the colors began to separate. When his vision cleared he saw Elle's flat hand hovering next to his chin.

"You aren't going to run away from this. I know you aren't the one to count on to give words of advice but the least you could do is actually be here with us. That is your best friend out there and you can't even pretend that you know how to help him."

Elle lowered her hand and slid back down the ladder.

"Nobody knows what to do, but that doesn't mean you don't do anything."

Boy nodded but remained in his bed next to his broken window.

"I am sorry for hitting you," she stopped to say, "but you deserved it."

The distant sounds of cabinets and drawers being thrown open and closed echoed into their room. Elle disappeared into the hallway to look for Leo. Moments later, Boy heard a flurry of heated exchanges followed by a piercing scream. Boy leaned forward and peered through the gap in the unclosed door. There was Leo, lying on his side, writhing on the ground, with a blue soapy liquid spilling from between his lips. Elle had thrown herself down beside him and was screaming out for help. Miss Jennie rushed out of her bedroom and tried to sit

Leo up against the wall. Elle threw Leo's arm around her shoulder, speaking steadily into his ear, as Miss Jennie ran to the phone.

Boy turned his head away to the broken window and the commotion blurred into an unnatural silence behind him. Boy's heart stuck in his chest as the chance to be a hero hung in the balance. He refused to react; he was paralyzed by his prophecy, fearful of failure, unwilling to accept that he did not know how to save someone.

A fierce gust of cold wind swirled through the street and a steady sheet of rain began to pour from the darkened sky. Boy focused his attention on the leaking clouds. His eyes obsessed over each singular splash that watered the concrete. He could see each drop so clearly that he could count the rain. Boy stuck his arm through the shattered window, persuaded by the raindrops to catch them before they fell, and cut himself on the jagged pieces of glass. His arm levitated in front of him as little droplets of blood bubbled from the scratches, rising like blooming roses in a garden. It was in that moment, as he watched the blood flowers drink in the falling rain, that he profoundly realized just how unpredictable the weather really was.

Chapter 8: Cloud Dancers

"I'm still too sad to cry," Elle said, pulling her head out of the half empty tub and sliding down onto the bathroom floor.

Boy rocked back and forth with his arms around his knees, tapping the back of his head against the cold toilet bowl. His journal was closed, resting on the corner of the sink, with a capped pen balanced on top of it.

"Do you ever cry, Boy?"

Boy shook his head.

"You should try it sometime."

Boy didn't acknowledge her.

"Life is such a hypocrite," Elle said. "I just hate when it makes no sense on purpose."

Elle stared up at the anxiety provoking flickering of the lightbulb.

"Part of me is surprised that he would want to take his life. He just isn't the type of person, if there is a type, but then I realize that they took his life away from him years ago. His life gave him away."

Elle scraped at the fading paint on her fingernails until the sound of the scratching made her paranoid. She placed her chin on the edge of the bathtub and stuck her hand into the water. She spread her fingers and watched them swim beneath the surface.

"I would really love to hear how you feel about this," Elle said.

There was a predictable silence. She curled her knuckles and made her fingers run in place.

"Nothing? You feel nothing? You wouldn't want to feel nothing."

Elle pulled her soggy fingertips out of the water and wiped her hand on her dress.

"I can't talk to myself about this."

Elle reached forward and stole Boy's journal off of the sink.

"If you aren't going to tell me how you feel then I will just have to read about how you feel," Elle said, flipping through the pages.

Boy stood up and snatched his book from Elle, who then jumped to her feet and yanked it back from him. Boy took a step forward and Elle met him halfway. She shoved the journal into Boy's chest and pressed her nose against his.

"I've already read this. If you want to be a hero so badly, be one."

Elle brushed past Boy and smacked down the switch to the flickering light.

"It's too quiet in here."

Tension had been high in the house all through the long night and into the break of the day. The air was thick and suffocating and there was nothing to distract from the deafening silence of Leo's absence. For Boy, the quiet was familiar, and he could escape it any time that he wanted. But Elle didn't want to escape, and the silence was not her friend. She was living in her own echo, and she was starting not to recognize the sound of her own voice.

Elle stood in the doorway of their bedroom with her hands pressed against the frame and looked at Leo's empty bed. On his pillow was a neat pile of his photos and papers that she had collected for him off of the floor. Next to her own bed was her suitcase, zipped and locked. She looked guiltily over her shoulder at Boy who was standing with his back against the wall and closed the bedroom door.

Elle walked up and down the long lonely hallway that split the house, stopping to contemplate the framed animal pictures as if it were her first time seeing them.

"A strange place to call home, isn't it?"

Boy shrugged.

"You don't call it home. You don't call it anything. You don't call anything, anything."

Elle's thoughts wandered with her as she roamed into the kitchen. She swung open and closed the loose hanging cabinets, observing her surroundings with a fascinated sense of novelty the way a tourist would admire a foreign land.

"I'm hot," she said, opening the empty fridge and sitting inside of it with her legs stretched out in front of her. The light from the fridge backlit Elle into a silhouette, reminding Boy of the night that she first knocked on their door.

"The hospital should let Leo come home in a week. Once they feel that he won't try to…harm himself anymore, they will let him go."

Elle shivered from the seeping chill of the fridge.

"Miss Jennie seems more disturbed by everything than you do, and she hates Leo."

Elle looked up at Boy and Boy looked down at Elle.

"Are you going to write this in your story? Or are you going to leave this part out?"

Boy's fingers dug into the leather cover of his journal.

"Would you rather be alone?" Elle provoked.

"Do you want me to leave too so you can be by yourself?"

Boy dropped his head, ashamed that his affections were being questioned. He assumed that his loyalties went without saying, though it was true that they had never been spoken.

"Today is the thirteenth you know, which means it's an unlucky day. Boy, sweet Boy, I want to tell you that we have something else that we need to talk about, but I am afraid it wouldn't be much of a conversation."

Elle rubbed the fresh goosebumps on her arm.

"Now, I am cold. And it's still too quiet."

Elle closed the fridge and hopped onto the counter next to an old antenna radio covered in dust. She picked up the radio and shook it clean, then stretched herself out to plug the tangled cord into the wall. Just then the doorbell rang and Elle pretended not to hear it. She quickly twisted the dials and skimmed through the stations of static before landing on the jazzy sounds of a saxophone. She cranked up the volume of the radio and a deep, smooth blues voice spoke calmly over the music.

"I think dancing is always the answer, don't matter what the question is," the radio voice said.

The doorbell rang again and Elle cringed.

"Dancing is therapy, it's the remedy, and it'll cure anything. Dancing is the sunrise, it's a hot shower on a winter day. Dancing is being wrapped in a blanket with your favorite book. It's hand written love letters, an intimate conversation, it's clean laundry, it's hand-made, fresh-baked, dancing is vacation and dancing is coming home…"

As the voice rode the waves of the music, Elle stole glances at Boy across the kitchen. Boy's body swayed slightly as his mind fixated on the front door. Elle slid down off the counter and approached him, placing the toes of her shoes against his. She tilted her head and rested her face against him to listen to him breathe. His chest rose slowly and fell quickly like an ancient empire. Together they rocked back and forth, their weight shifting gently from one foot to the other.

"Dancing is gratitude, it's forgiveness, it's appreciation, it's respect, it's patience. Dancing is passion, dancing is *com*-passion, it's humility, it's authenticity. Dancing is a virtue and virtuous. But dancing can be mysterious, a mystery, yes dancing is full of secrets, but I can share those secrets."

Boy tightened his arms around Elle's waist.

"The first thing you must know is that it's not the music, but it's the people dancing along beside you that move you. It is connection through expression – human to human synergy vibrating through the air you breathe. That is the 'why' of dancing, but the 'how' is another secret, and that secret is simple: When you dance you have to dance like you are dancing on clouds. You have to step soft, softer than soft. Can you imagine that?"

Boy could imagine it, and so he did. His eyes began to spin and he slid his hands into Elle's. She could feel the familiar rush of fantasy's colors flooding her body. The kitchen walls folded down like a cardboard box and the dancers' feet lifted off of the ground as they rose together into the sky. Elle looked down at the house disappearing below them and could feel the mist of the clouds on the back of her neck.

Elle pulled a hand away from Boy and stuck a finger into the air.

"I have the perfect poem for this." Elle stepped onto Boy's feet and leaned backwards.

"Eyes closed and minds open
They floated,
With heart shaped balloons as big as the moon and redder than roses

Tied to their wrists like a bow on a gift,
Winds of young hope what an effortless drift,
Small scientists' hypothesis of gravity's myth,
They mixed the freedom of youth inside of a magical potion
With love, what a potent component,
Cotton candy clouds rolling above the waves of an ocean,
The silent emotions of a poet unspoken
Causing quite the commotion,
The sleeping bird sings the chorus of the orphans,
Who dance while they circle in orbit,
Unafraid of the atmospheric forces and pressure,
For if they can't float for infinity,
Then blissfully,
They can fall for forever together."

As Elle finished reciting her poem she grabbed Boy by the waist and dipped him. They lost their balance and began to tumble down through the clouds. They laughed and swam through the sky until they landed softly on their backs.

"I wrote that poem for us the first day I met you," Elle said, staring at the clouds that Boy was shifting into abstract shapes above their heads.

"You need to finish that story," Elle said, blowing apart the clouds with her breath.

"It deserves an ending." Elle flattened her velvet dress with her hands. She noticed that her finger nails were painted a vibrant purple with white polka-dots. Elle could feel her face warming.

"Did I ever tell you about my old house? The one that I lived in when I was adopted?"

Boy crossed his arms across his chest and shook his head.

"It is my favorite place in the world," Elle reached out and put her hand on Boy's elbow, just to be touching him.

"It's not a big house but it's not a small house either. It only has one floor and a basement. The house is white, the door is red, and the roof is black and pointy." As Elle spoke the house began to take shape in the cloud in front of her. "There is a small stone path that goes from the street to the front steps and they are all different sizes. We have a golden puppy that plays in the yard and gets stuck in the bushes and we have a metal mailbox stuck into the ground next to a skinny tree, maybe the skinniest tree you have ever seen. It might be the skinniest tree in the world."

Elle admired the nebulous image of her old home across from her.

"It isn't that far from here. All you have to do is cross the city. I remember the car ride coming here. I wanted to watch exactly where we were going so I would know how to get back home. We didn't turn once; we just went from one end to the other. I don't know how long it would take but if you had enough time you would eventually get there. All you have to do is go straight. You wouldn't get lost."

Elle let her hand slide off of Boy and stood up solemnly. She pushed down her dress and took a step towards the floating house made of clouds. Elle lifted her hand to her face and held up her eyelid. With one finger she carefully pressed against the surface of her eye and her vision blurred. Glimpses of light from Miss Jennie's kitchen snuck around the dispersed colors. Elle pulled her hand away and blinked, rubbing her eyelid with the back of her hand.

"Everything will be the same as you remembered it, when you finally come home," Elle said as Boy sat up straight.

"That is what Miss Jennie wrote on the back of one of her photographs. I think her sister was in a coma and never woke up."

Elle mumbled something to herself, walked down the path through the yard and stood facing the front door of the house of clouds.

"Will that be us, Boy?" Elle asked under her breath.

A drop of color rolled down Boy's cheek.

"Waiting for someone who is never coming back?"

She put her hand on the doorknob and outstretched the other behind her. Elle's arm shook and she pounded her foot on the imaginary steps, demanding permission to leave. When Boy finally accepted the moment for what it was — a goodbye — he placed her white suitcase in her empty hand. Elle gave the handle a familiar squeeze, pushed open the door, and disappeared.

Chapter 9: Home Alone

Boy knew pain, but this was an unfamiliar form of suffering. Elle's absence haunted him on both sides of his mind, for in his fantasy she was always by his side, which served as a constant and cruel reminder that in reality she was not. He tortured himself with visions of her leaving, forcing her to speak final words that were not her own. She would be there and then be gone, vanishing again and again like a clichéd magician's trick. Boy was chasing a ghost in his memory, never allowing himself to catch her. He was obsessed with the longing, imagining her in ways that she never was. He continued to create worlds for her – tragic masterpieces, homages of fidelity that she would never see. There was nothing he wouldn't imagine for her.

Every time his eyes stopped spinning he saw the emptiness that surrounded him and would seek company within himself once more. Life had never been easy for Boy, but in these moments it was harder than it had ever been. It was in these times that the words of Mr. Man echoed louder than ever before. The idea of disappearing deeper into an invented existence was undeniably enticing, but Boy forced himself to shake away the thoughts with contempt. Elle's words also spoke to him in his isolation; she had understood him and convinced him that in order to be a hero, he must simply be one. She did not doubt that he would become one, but the questions that remained were hindersome. Who exactly would he save, and how?

"I'm back from vacation," Leo's raspy voice called from the doorway.

"I'm not as tan as I thought I would be."

Leo smiled a weak smile and folded his hands behind his back. Boy scaled down the ladder and rushed to greet him. There was an awkward moment in which neither of the boys knew how to embrace the other, and after a few hesitant pats on shoulders and backs Boy and Leo stepped apart.

"I've been practicing saying that in my head all week," Leo said.

"First time saying it out loud though, didn't want them to think I was…" Leo hesitated, "…crazy," he finished.

Boy's eyes flicked to the floor.

"It was pretty good right? Unexpected given the circumstances and everything. I don't know how I feel about my voice though. Miss Jennie says I sound like a GPS with strep throat."

Boy let out a noise that was a confusing mix of a snort and a cough as he choked down an unacceptable laugh.

"It actually is pretty clever. I hate to give her any credit for anything at all, but it is a fairly accurate description."

Leo walked over to his bed and saw his photos and papers stacked neatly in a pile.

"I heard Elle was re-adopted. I didn't even know that was possible," Leo said, shuffling through the photos.

"Imagine being loved so much that people fight to keep you and then fight to get you back when they lose you. We can't relate, but good for her."

Leo turned to Boy and scratched his head.

"How do you feel about that? About Elle leaving? I feel like it all happened so fast. Are you okay?"

Leo seemed as uncomfortable asking the question as Boy felt trying to find an answer to it. No, he was not okay, but it was almost too simple to express.

"I didn't want to die," Leo said bluntly, turning his shoulders away from Boy.

"I still don't want to die," he added. "Maybe I just wanted to feel like I was going to die."

The elephant in the room was now naked. Boy wanted to walk away. It wasn't just that he didn't know what to say, he didn't even know how to hear what Leo was saying.

"Or maybe I just wanted someone else to feel like I was going to die."

Leo shrugged and Boy shrugged back with his hand on his stomach. He felt uneasy. It was his responsibility to show Leo that his life was valued but he had no words to do so.

Leo rummaged through their small closet, pulling out a dust-covered duffle bag that had been buried at the bottom. Boy took a step back to give him space and shoved his hands in his pocket.

"My father…" Leo started, then stopped, grabbing and rubbing his singed throat. "My father was always disappointed that I wasn't better at math. I wasn't bad at math, I was a little kid. I was counting on my fingers the only way I knew how, but my dad wanted me to be some sort of savant. I wasn't. So I took it personally. I became obsessed with being good at math and now I'm great at math." Leo paced around the room collecting his belongings and placing them carefully in his bag.

"The one concept that has always confused me, though, is the difference between real numbers and imaginary numbers. People debate whether zero is a real number and I never understood how it could be. Zero is nothing, nothing is not real, but some say zero is real. Doesn't make sense." Leo looked at Boy for confirmation, who nodded in agreement that it did not make sense.

"But I think I finally get it now. I did some calculations you know, and I calculated that I have zero people that love me. Zero people love me, which is actually different than having nobody because nobody never existed. Out of all the people who do exist, zero of them love me, which makes zero a very real number."

Leo stopped packing his things and stared at Boy.

"I know one person who loves me and I am going to see him, because one is greater than zero."

Leo pushed his glasses up onto his nose.

"I am going to find my father, he is going to love me, he will apologize for what he did, I will forgive him, and you already know what will happen after that." Leo pointed to the sky with his index finger.

He bent over and zipped up his duffle bag and Boy took another step away from him.

"The plan is simple. I sneak out, I find the train station just outside of the city, follow the tracks west because I don't have money for a ticket, and then I follow the river that runs right to the edge of the lab where I think my father still works. I will wait for him in the parking lot and when he sees me he will realize that I am ready to go with him. I know it isn't flawless, but any plan is better than no plan."

Leo pushed his bag across the floor next to the bedroom door with his foot.

"I am leaving at midnight."

The clock on the wall read 9:43 pm.

"You coming with me?"

A disheartening silence followed Leo's hopeful question.

"Okay."

Leo sat down on his duffle bag and Boy climbed the ladder of the bunk bed to stare out of the crooked window. All of the lights in the house across the street were off. There were no cars in the driveway and the curtains to the windows were closed. With no one else's life to watch, Boy was forced to reflect upon his own.

Every great hero has a great adventure, but he was not a great hero and thus had no great adventure. Perhaps the adventure creates the hero from nothing, or maybe they form together at each step of the journey. Maybe heroics were just exaggerated normalcy, everyday hyperbole. *What was the opposite of a hero*, Boy wondered. Whatever he was, was the opposite. Whoever he was. Boy was struggling to remember why he even wanted to be a hero at all.

"I thought about your mom the other day," Leo called out with his chin resting on his folded knuckles. Boy turned and stared at him.

"I know I have never met her. I don't know what she even looks like, but when I pictured her she had eyes like you. Miss Jennie told me that she was in a psych ward. Maybe she was lying, but being in that hospital having to prove to everyone that I wasn't mental, it was awful. I don't know if your mom is actually crazy or not. I know how long she has been away, but I feel bad for her, because in there they make you feel crazy even if you aren't. Their questions, the way they look at you, it makes you paranoid." Leo glanced up and made eye contact with Boy and the both of them looked away.

"To be honest, thinking about your mom helped convince me to break out of here and go find my father. I almost felt guilty when I was coming up with the plan because it's foolish. I felt like I was justifying them keeping me in there for having those thoughts. But it doesn't matter what anyone else might think it is because it's what I am going to do. In my head you were going to come with me to see my father and then all of us would go to visit your mother, wherever she is."

Leo clapped his hands together. "That's how I saw it in my head, but we don't live in there, do we?"

We could, Boy thought to himself, already imagining a world for their family to exist.

"Why don't you go see your mother?" Leo asked, his question snapping Boy from his trance.

"You know you could but you don't want to. I will never understand that."

Leo stared at Boy, whose eyes danced around him like a bandit dodging bullets at his feet.

"Here I am, ready to run away to try and find my father, to do whatever it takes to see him again, and you won't even walk down that hallway and ask Miss Jennie where your mother is. No one is stopping you from seeing her. You are stopping you and it makes me sad."

Boy turned his back to Leo and looked once more to the window, but saw nothing. His focus was inward. It was true that Boy did not want to see his mother and it was true that he fought away thoughts of her. He had ostracized his own hero and the reason was painfully buried beneath layers of scar tissue. In his heart of hearts he knew that he loved her. He knew that she had sacrificed everything for him. So maybe it wasn't true that he didn't want to see her, but he didn't want her to see him. Boy didn't want his mother to see that he had not become the hero he had promised to be. Boy had not just failed her once; he failed her every single day that he failed to save someone else.

It was a bludgeoning disgrace. It was a beating he had grown accustomed to, but refused to accept any longer. If Boy was to be a hero; he could not be his own enemy.

"I am leaving. I don't want to wait any longer. I have almost died here twice. This will not be my cemetery."

Leo stood at the end of the burnt rainbow on the wall.

"I will see you again someday," he said, closing his fingers tightly around the handles of his duffle bag. "Somewhere in the sky."

Leo turned to go as dramatically as planned, when he was stopped by the unexpected sound of the wooden ladder creaking behind him. When he turned back around there was Boy, standing at his side with his backpack slung over his shoulder and his mother's red bandana wrapped in his hand. Boy gave half a smile and Leo smiled the other half for him.

"You should wear it," Leo said, pointing to the bandana. "There is never a real reason to wear a bandana, but that has never stopped anyone from doing it."

Boy rubbed his fingers on the worn cloth reminiscently. He questioned whether he deserved to wear the bandana. It had belonged to a real hero. He had not earned the title or the honor. Wearing another's cape could not make him fly, but perhaps it could inspire flight. This would be his defining decision; the first step in destiny's direction.

Boy rolled the bandana tightly across his legs then raised it high, placing it gently over his head like a crown of thorns. He tied the cloth into a tight knot and lowered his hands ceremoniously to his sides.

"I don't know what will happen next, but no matter what happens it will be better than nothing happening to us," Leo promised.

He checked the time. It was barely 10pm.

"I don't really know why I said midnight, we can leave whenever really. I just felt like midnight is kind of like the standard adventure start time. We don't even have to leave tonight, tomorrow is just as good, but I figured we get on with it, rip it off like a bandage."

Both boys looked around the room to see if they had forgotten anything while simultaneously hoping they would forget everything.

"I did my best to destroy it," Leo laughed, and so did Boy, despite knowing that it was far from a joke.

They snuck out of their room and down the hallway, pausing subconsciously to stare at the glowing light seeping out from under Miss Jennie's door. The two boys gave each other subtle nods to acknowledge that they were finally going to leave Miss Jennie in the past, right where she wanted to be left. By the time they reached the front door and stopped to take one last look at 84 D, the house they never called home, they were both emotional. It was an experience that they had constantly begged to come to an end, but now that the end had come it seemed surreal.

Sentiment aside, it was time to say a proper goodbye.

"I will never come back," Leo promised, opening the door for Boy.

Whether Leo knew it or not at the time, he would be a man of his word. Neither he nor Boy would ever step foot inside of 84 D again. For better or worse, they would find out soon enough.

Chapter 10: Trash Mountain

Walking along those infinite train tracks under the high-noon sun seemed like a metaphor to Boy. Perhaps it was an analogy of guidance, an allusion to limitless adventure, or a personification of the predetermined path that one follows blindly through life. The entire scene was a symbol of something. As Boy balanced atop the metal rails, placing one foot in front of the other, he debated what the world was trying to tell him.

"I feel like we should be whistling," Leo said from the other side of the tracks.

"In all of the great adventure stories, at the beginning of the quest, they either sing or whistle. If we were two fictional characters in a book, we would be whistling right now."

Boy gave Leo two short whistles to humor him as he lost his balance and hopped into the middle of the track.

"If you were a bird those would have been your first words," Leo said proudly.

Leo opened up his chest and inhaled the fresh air of freedom.

"This is why non-fiction is better than fiction. You can feel this; you don't have to imagine it. Whatever happens, happens, and you are attached to it because it is happening. You can't be skeptical. There is no debate about what should or could have been because you are experiencing what was experienced. You have to be out here to know what it is really like out here. Do you understand what I am saying, Boy? How are you going to sit in a dark room and describe the sun? You have to feel it on your face; you have to let it burn your skin. You have to live a great story to tell a great story. How could you tell me what it feels like to stand with your feet on these tracks if you have never been near a train?"

Leo looked back over his shoulder as he felt the rumble beneath his feet. The iron face of the approaching train revealed itself through the ripples of dry heat in the distance. The boys stepped to the side and watched the train pass by with great respect. Boy continued to ponder metaphors and wondered if the train was supposed to represent freedom, or at least the feeling of freedom, but questioned if a train was free if it was confined to its tracks. Then again, one could build a track anywhere. Trains traveled across the entire world. How could one be freer than a train? Symbolism was complicated.

As Boy was contemplating deeper meanings, Leo had wandered ahead and was peering into an opening in the bushes. They had traveled throughout the night and were greeted warmly by the rising sun. The day had come to life before their eyes and energy was high and the atmosphere was liberating.

"Boy," Leo called out, waving for his attention from the gap in the brush.

Discarded off to the side of the tracks was a crippled black coupe with its flat tires melted to the rocks beneath it. The body of the car was crumpled like a soda can and the windows were cracked into spiderwebs of glass.

"I think it might be too late to try to catch a ride with them," Leo said, sticking his thumb in the air like a hitchhiker.

"Then again they probably weren't too great with directions if they ended up here."

Leo dropped his thumb as a darker thought crashed into him.

"Do you think someone parked it on the tracks? To, you know…" Leo asked, running his fingers horizontally across his throat.

Boy didn't need to be a mechanic to assess that the car was totaled; therefore, it was not much of a stretch to assume that it had been hit by a train.

"Do you think there is a dead body inside?" Leo asked.

Boy shot him a disillusioned stare and turned his back to the wreckage. If there was or wasn't, Boy was not interested in finding out. Leo's sudden fascination with mortality was off-putting, given the recency of his own brush with death. Leo, however, did not share Boy's reservations. He put his face against the cracked window and scoped around.

"It's dirty, but nobody is dead in there," Leo said.

Boy could tell that he was disappointed.

Leo tapped on the glass with his finger. "I *do* see a $20 bill in there that needs us to save it."

Boy peered in the window and cupped his hands to block the sun. The money was stuffed into the gap between the seats, dried and wrinkled like a raisin in the sun. Leo yanked at the door and the handle broke off in his hand.

"There must be a child lock," Leo said, laughing prematurely at his own joke. He traded the door handle for a large round rock from the ground and cocked it back behind his head.

"Is this stealing?" Leo lowered the rock momentarily.

"I mean, I am probably still going to break this window and take it, but before I do I want to know if I should feel bad about it."

Leo put his hands on his hips.

"Technically, the money doesn't belong to anyone. It would belong to whoever owned the car but it's an abandoned car, so no one owns it, which means no one owns the stuff that is inside it. I know it is not mine, but it is nobody's, and you can't steal from nobody."

Leo raised the rock and threw it through the window. The glass shattered around his feet and he reached carefully through the jagged opening and retrieved the crumpled bill by its corner.

"Now, it's ours," Leo said.

"Legally," he added.

Boy was intrigued by Leo's recklessness. They had lived nearly the entirety of their lives in self-imposed captivity, subdued and tranquilized by fear and isolation. They deserved to be wild.

As Leo started to walk away from the potential crime scene he saw Boy standing armed with a rock of his own, tossing it up and spinning it around his fingers.

"That's right. Destroy it," Leo instructed.

Boy didn't need directions. He launched the rock through the front windshield and watched with sickening satisfaction as it smashed to pieces. Boy scooped up another rock and tossed it to Leo, who did the honor of flinging it through the back window. The boys took turns breaking everything that was breakable and then admired the damage they had done. Boy felt the destructive surge from the rocks beneath his feet flow through him.

Boy was dangerous.

Leo too could feel the energy of their newfound freedom. He finally had the space to walk with the confidence he always knew he had. With unlimited, unknown potential for opportunity around him, Leo was in his element.

"We didn't get to choose how this all started for us, and we might not be able to choose how it all ends, but we can control this. For once, I just want to have a say in my own life. I shouldn't have to beg for that, I won't beg, not anymore."

Leo started up as if he had more to say but shook his head and walked away. Boy knew that most of the words he spoke were from the books he read, but there was not a single plagiarized emotion in his voice. Boy was proud to be Leo's friend, and he knew that Leo was proud to be his. These were the type of conversations that freedom carried.

The two travelers continued on in inspired silence, each with their own thoughts, taking in the surroundings. It was a beautiful day to be a rebellious outcast in search of belonging, and with the persistent sun as their witness they vowed not to slow until their journey was complete. The boys felt one with nature; their senses were on high alert, but they began to question if they were too attuned to the earth when a foul smell ambushed their noses. At first it was shocking, and then it became outright offensive. It smelled like warm, decomposing death. The boys were both repulsed and naturally fascinated. They followed the smell with twisted pleasure and were led through the bushes to a chain link fence that had fallen flat on the ground. The boys stepped over the fence like a welcome mat and entered into an isolated world of garbage. It was a sprawling expanse of rubbish that defied even the dirtiest expectations one would have for a dump.

It was almost remarkable in a revolting and repugnant way to Boy, who stood in awe amongst the steaming piles of garbage and the swirling stench. Leo had disappeared, rummaging through the waste, and Boy felt as if the world had ended. It seemed like a cynical foreshadow, a small scale apocalypse; if all that was, were to no longer be, it would become exactly this. The desolation was disheartening and frightening, but Leo, as usual, had his own, more positive interpretation of the circumstances.

"It's like an amusement park when you think about it," Leo called from out of sight. Boy turned his head on a swivel to locate his voice, squinting through the mirage-like waves of heat that were circulating.

"You have bumper cars," Leo hollered, as Boy saw a rusted shopping cart dart out in front of him, wobble frantically and then crash violently into a thick piece of scrap metal. The cart landed upside down, stranded on its back like a shelled animal, with the wheels spinning furiously going no place at all.

"We have concession stands," Leo said, emerging from behind a stack of crates overflowing with deteriorating fruits. The decaying produce had been organized in a series of perfect, sagging pyramids, surrounded by a plague-like cloud of flies that were taking turns crash-landing on the molded skin of the fruit. Boy's stomach rumbled slightly.

"There are carnival games," Leo said, picking up a coverless baseball and tossing it up in the air. He distanced himself from the crates of stacked fruit and slung the baseball towards them. The ball smashed through the center of a drooping orange which splashed to the ground with its juices leaking out of its sides. Boy raised his eyebrows at Leo, impressed, and Leo shrugged at his accuracy.

"Over there it looks like we have a fun house." Leo pointed off to their side where there was an empty shipping container from which a parade of rats was scurrying in and out. The incessant scratching of nails against the metal surface reverberated maniacally from the dark receptacle, giving cause for Boy and Leo to take a few cautious steps in the opposite direction.

That's when they saw it.

"The main attraction," Leo said, craning his neck to try and see the top.

"Trash Mountain."

Towering above their park of filth was a mammoth mass of trash piled to a point that nearly pierced the clouds. It was a natural wonder of the underworld, a monument of waste; a pious pillar to bow down to, or to climb up. Boy and Leo marveled at the structure. It could have passed for a work of the ancient gods, an inexplicable curiosity that lives for eternity through myths and legends. The two boys looked at each other and then once more to their surroundings. They were alone. This was their discovery.

In silent competitive agreement, the two raced up the mountain with a sudden burst of movement and grunted laughter. Boy and Leo hurried their way to the top, clambering over broken appliances, workout equipment, and outdated furniture. The steeper they climbed, the deeper their legs submerged beneath the sea of debris soaking their socks and shoes. Boy beat Leo to the peak by two lewd lunges and put his hands on his hips, trying to catch his breath and filter the air he was breathing simultaneously.

From above, they could smell the trash cooking beneath their feet. It was a sickening scent, but the view from the top made Boy feel grandiose. It was such an unfamiliar feeling that he didn't know how to process it, nor could he recall a time where he had felt such a sensation before. As Boy pondered this newfound feeling of importance, Leo shook off a large paper that had stuck to the sole of his shoe. He scraped off the clinging scrap with the heel of his foot, but realized that it was the corner of a much larger piece of canvas that was buried beneath the trash.

Leo whipped out the canvas like he was shaking off a sandy towel at the beach, and when all of the trash had slid off of the top, a beautiful painting was revealed from below. There was a woman painted in a field of yellow flowers and all of the lines were hazy and smudged. She was a blur, as if she had been moving too quickly for the artist to capture her. The woman had a subtle smile on a soft face and her hand seemed to wave at the two boys admiring her from their mountain of trash.

"This is such a shame really," Leo said, holding the canvas up to the sun. "This might be someone's masterpiece. Someone might have dedicated their whole life to it and it ended up in a pile of garbage."

Boy thought it was a wonderful portrait. Everything about it was lovely except the place it was hung, or rather, the place it had fallen.

"Who is to say what art belongs in a museum and what belongs in the trash?" Leo asked.

"Just because we found it in the garbage doesn't mean that it is garbage."

Boy thought that Leo was going to delve into another life lesson that he had extracted from the story of a stranger, as he was always searching for the opportunity to apply them to his own, but his thoughts carried him away from the painting.

Leo surveyed the compost paradise.

"I feel like I am on a stage. It makes me want to give a speech."

Leo scanned the audience of garbage with pride.

"Everyone practices acceptance speeches, except for maybe you, Boy, who doesn't practice speech at all," Leo said.

"Everyone wants to be ready to say thank you for their award when the time comes, even if they don't actually think they will win one. Or maybe everyone thinks they will, one day."

Boy liked to believe that he would win an award, but even for him, that was hard to imagine.

Leo looked above him and took an empty swipe at the clouds that drifted overhead. They seemed like they were right there, within reach, but then again, clouds always seemed like one could touch them.

He shook his head and let the painting fall off the side of the mountain, drifting and flipping out of sight and out of mind.

"This is the closest I have ever been to space," Leo said, looking from his feet to the sky above him.

Boy looked up. They still seemed pretty far away.

Chapter 11: River Rabbit

They had reached the end of infinity and it was a river, infinite in its own respect. The train tracks had ended and were replaced by the steadfast flow of water. The trees that lined the river's bank softened and spotted the sun, leaving patches of golden, heavenly light spread across their path. The river did not seem to connect to the outer world. It conveyed through its idyllic ambience that it existed independently, an endless loop of sacred water running in place. The atmosphere was pensive, making it easy to become lost within one's thoughts, but Boy made an effort to remain present. He tried to stop his mind from imagining that he was there, so that he could fully embrace actually being there. The more Boy forced himself to appreciate the moment, the more he felt that he was missing it completely.

The change of scenery was a shock to his system. He was finally on the other side of the window. For the first time in a long time, Boy was in a new world and didn't have to fabricate it inside of his imagination. There was peace in that.

Boy found the reflection of his eyes in the shimmering water. He wondered how long he could watch the river run before it ran dry. The river would lose its water long after Boy had died of thirst, he decided. Boy laughed at the irony of the imagery, his shriveled body lying patiently next to a fountain of life. Then he laughed again because he wasn't sure if it was ironic or not.

Speaking of dying of thirst, Boy was convinced that the blood-sucking mosquitoes that were feasting upon him would never suffer that same fate. Their river utopia, although precious, was infested with hovering vampire dragons that stalked their every step. No matter how many they sent to their splattering death, there was always another legion of mosquitos waiting to take a sip. The boys' desperation bred creativity, as they began concocting schemes to outsmart the insects.

"I am going to spit in my palm, they will all gather around like animals at a watering hole, and then I will clap them out of existence," Leo said.

Leo put his plan into motion but the mosquitos did not bite; figuratively, that is, because physically they continued to eat him alive. Leo wiped his hand on his pants.

"What if I stay perfectly still and let them all land on me, give them a false sense of security, and then you run up and smack them all when they least expect it?"

Boy was only half listening to Leo's strategy and half paranoid by the daunting buzzing that was tickling his ear. The mosquitoes were very friendly with him, but they really loved Leo. They swarmed his head like children around an ice cream truck. His arms and neck were red and swollen.

"I look like a kid with severe food allergies who sniffed a peanut," Leo said.

Boy couldn't complain, because as miserable as the mosquitoes were making them, he still wouldn't want to be anywhere else. Kids their age were supposed to be trekking by a river, sweating and being bitten by bugs. Boy just wished that he had been bitten by more bugs in his lifetime.

"This just goes to show you that we would not last long in the wilderness. We just don't have the survival skills," Leo said, tripping over a stick.

Boy couldn't argue with that.

"What would we do if we ran into a bear?" Leo asked.

Boy scratched his head. He didn't realize he was supposed to have prepared a plan for that possibility.

"I would probably just choke it out, depending on its angle of attack."

Leo picked up the large stick he had stepped on.

"Or I could shove this through a honeycomb and then throw it like a spear as far away from us as I could. The bear would chase it and it would give us time to run. Theoretically that is."

Boy struggled to picture the strategy succeeding in even the best case scenario. He didn't share Leo's same confidence in the theory.

"It's good to have options in those types of situations," Leo said.

Just then, there was a rustling of leaves from behind a pair of trees. The two boys stopped in their tracks and Leo turned to head in the opposite direction. Without further warning, the hidden creature hopped into the open in front of them and then hopped again and again. The river resident was a fat fluffy bunny rabbit. The bunny was so soft and furry that they could barely see its big cartoonish eyes or its silly buckteeth. Its fur was like a scoop of ice cream, chocolate mixed with caramel, and it had oversized vanilla feet. The rabbit bounced back and forth, darting playfully towards them and then jumping out of reach.

"You thought it was a bear didn't you? You were so scared," Leo teased, crouching down to greet the rabbit.

"How are we supposed to play with it? Does it fetch?" Leo asked.

He picked up a twig off of the ground and flung it next to the river. The rabbit stood up on its back legs and gave a peep around and then dropped back down and sniffed the grass.

"It is like a living cotton ball," Leo said.

He held out his hand, stretching his fingers towards the bunny.

"I need to touch it."

The rabbit's head bobbed spastically from side to side like a cornered boxer, then gave one hop backwards, out of Leo's reach.

"I would try to feed it but I don't want to accidentally give it poisonous berries or something. I'm just going to assume you don't have a carrot on you."

Boy patted his empty pockets.

"Do you know what poison ivy looks like?"

Boy shook his head.

"Well, then I'm not going to try and make it a salad," Leo said.

Leo inched closer to the rabbit with his hand extended, shuffling his feet beneath him, but the bunny shied away. As Boy watched Leo stalk after the playful rabbit he imagined that Elle was beside him by the river. She sat coyly with her legs crossed beneath her and her hands folded on top of her lavender dress. Her dark olive skin radiated beneath the soft glow of the sun's diffused rays and her aura was reminiscent of that of a mythical nymph. She seemed to represent a chameleon paradox – everywhere she went she both blended into yet stood out from her environment. Boy wondered if he was imagining her to be more beautiful than she was, but then quickly remembered that she was more beautiful than he could ever imagine. Elle waited patiently for Boy to give her words to speak, but he was not sure what she would say. He only knew what he would want her to say.

"I told you it wasn't easy being original," she said.

Elle tilted her face to the daylight like a sunflower.

"You should be with him right now, trying to pet that rabbit. This is a real adventure, Boy, you don't need to use your imagination for this," she said.

Boy watched fondly as Leo crawled on his hands and knees trying to get close enough to give the rabbit a touch.

"I know you miss me, Boy, but I am here with you even when you feel like you've forgotten me. That is what you wanted me to say, isn't it?"

Boy nodded bashfully and Elle pulled tight the shoelace that held up her hair.

"I want to tell you one thing about dreams, Boy, while you two are out here chasing them. There are going to be people who try to tell you what is and isn't possible, but it is never the ones who make their dreams come true that tell you that you can't do it. It is all of the people who killed their dreams to save themselves; they are the ones who want you to think that you can't both survive."

Boy thought of Mr. Man in his mansion and wondered which group of dreamers he belonged to.

"This is everyone's first time through life, nobody knows how it will end. Everyone is just taking their best guess. Don't let anyone else guess for you."

Elle said what she came to say and gave Boy a long drawn out wink.

"Tell Leo that I miss him, or at least give him a wave for me," she said with a wave of her own as she left Boy to his adventure.

Just as Leo was about to pet the friendly rabbit, an unfriendly mosquito landed on his arm. He slapped at the mosquito, missed it completely, and scared the rabbit back into the trees. He let himself fall over and Boy took a seat on a mossy rock next to him. Leo wrapped his arms around his legs and watched the water.

"Stupid rabbit," Leo said under his breath.

Boy had a feeling that Leo was nervous, that he saw this river as the final stretch of the journey. The finish line was not far away and Boy assumed that Leo was as anxious about not crossing it as he was about what would await him on the other side.

Leo dug his fingers into his head and grunted.

"I wish I could flip myself inside-out so people would know what was going on inside of me without me having to explain it."

Leo closed his eyes. The calming sounds of the river filled the hush of introspection. Boy loved to listen to Leo speak his mind; it was such a comfort to be able to breathe in fresh thoughts, as opposed to recycling the stale air of his own ideas.

"I feel like I am having an identity crisis," Leo said, ruffling his hair restlessly with his fingers.

"The only thing I have ever wanted is to go back to my father and now I can't think of a single reason why. The idea of going to space with him is the only thing that has kept me going, but now it just seems so ugly. He isn't a good person. I love him, but he was never good to me. He really believed that his contributions to science could change the world, and maybe they will one day, or maybe they already have. I wouldn't know, but everyone in his life was a necessary sacrifice."

Leo began to speak in a detached, factual sort of way that was unlike him.

"I don't think my parents ever really loved each other. The more I look at our old photos the more I can tell they were just posing for the pictures. I don't even think my dad really wanted to go to space, I just think he wanted to get as far away from us as possible."

A silence followed where only the sounds of the river spoke.

"He wanted to be a genius. I take that back – all he wanted was for everyone else to call him one. I will never call him a genius. He didn't know how to be a good father. He didn't know anything."

Leo stood and gave a long shrug. It was the type of shrug that only a person whose only option in life was to shrug, could shrug.

"And then I think that maybe I was too young to understand and that I have it all wrong."

Leo walked over to the edge of the river, dragging his feet.

"I just need to go to space with him one time, so I can move on. Then I will be free, free from my dream."

Boy thought of the unfinished journal in his backpack. He wanted to save his best friend. That was the ending that was meant to be. From Boy's perspective, their fates were irreversibly intertwined. There was no way out, only up. The thought alone made him nervous; knowing how special of a person Leo would be out in the world put immense pressure on Boy to make sure that he was given the opportunity. Forcing fate was easy in a fantasy, but this was far from that.

Boy thought of death, not often, but in that moment, and how a person could spend their whole life planning their final words and never get the chance to say them. Boy lived a heavy-hearted life.

He escaped from his thoughts as he saw Leo crouched down in front of him, looking around suspiciously.

"Do you think the police are looking for us?"

Boy nodded. They most likely were.

"If they find us, Boy, I am not going back."

Boy wondered what Leo really meant to say. He also wondered if Leo knew what he was really saying.

"They don't want to find us," Leo said. "We've been missing our whole lives. There is no reason to come for us now."

Just then, another mysterious rustle came from behind the trees. If this time it actually were a bear, Boy still had not come up with a strategy to survive. The two boys turned and were poised to run, but there was no need after all. To their most pleasant surprise, the friendly rabbit had returned, bringing with it two smaller bunnies hopping by its side. The furry family jumped around in circles and then passed through the legs of Leo to reach the edge of the river. Leo reached down and gave all three of them a pet as quickly as possible before they ran off. He looked to Boy with his mouth hanging open.

"Did you see that?"

Boy flicked his eyebrows up to the top of his forehead.

"I take back what I said. I called the rabbit stupid. I was wrong. That rabbit is a genius."

The two boys celebrated their little victory with no one in the world watching. They were alone again. They were alone together. Just two boys and a river.

Chapter 12: Royal Cheese

Night had returned uninvited. The angelic light that had filtered softly through the trees had disappeared and the unwelcomed darkness had taken its place. It was blindingly dark and there was nothing to salvage from the shadows. It had become too dangerous to even walk. The boys tripped and collided with one another as they tried to track the river's deceptive twists and turns. The hazards ultimately brought them to a halt, for they figured it safest to strategize standing still.

Leo had not anticipated seeing the sun set on them. The maps he had seen had made him believe that the journey would be simple and swift, but the approximated distances seemed to stretch further off of the paper. They had no food or shelter and the only resources they possessed were the water from the river and the crumpled $20 bill in Leo's pocket. It was difficult for them to see a way out, but then again it was difficult for them to see anything at all. When they looked down they couldn't even see their feet beneath them, but when they looked up they saw an answer. Floating in the distance, hundreds of feet above them, was a glowing crown made up of flashing lights. Neither of the boys believed much in divine signs, but whatever that thing in the sky was, they were meant to see it.

The two boys carefully climbed the river bank and found themselves at the edge of an empty lot of a shopping center. The plaza was littered with light poles and lonely parked cars, but none of the stores were open. The boys looked around distrustfully before vigilantly making their way to the source of the glowing light in the sky. Boy and Leo weaved through the buildings and stopped in the middle of a closed off street. There it was, the royal hat, radiating kingliness upon them. They craned their necks to look up at it. It seemed extravagant and out of place, true to noble form. The floating crown also came with a medieval castle below, bourgeois in its own inauthentic regard. It was comprised of a fake wooden drawbridge, dizzying cardboard minarets, plastic turrets modeled after chess pieces, and a moat which was nothing more than a roped off dirty puddle. The castle was painted all white and exhaled grease from its poorly disguised chimney.

'Burger Palace' was etched into a standing wooden sign at the end of the bridge. The two boys eyed and sniffed the castle curiously. They looked across to the other side of the street and saw a shady motel with the door wedged open by a garbage can. A hand-written sign was propped in one of the windows that read, 'Prices Negotiable.' The boys turned back to their enticingly lit castle and then back to the motel. It was as if heaven and hell were neighbors. They wanted to see what God was cooking.

The boys made their two-step journey across the drawbridge and reached the adorned entrance of their fast-food palace. A set of heavy wooden doors were pulled open before them by two teenage employees dressed like jesters, awaiting their arrival. The workers gave servile bows and two braces-filled smiles as the boys entered the palace. Boy and Leo had just returned to the renaissance. Gothic art hung haphazardly across the walls, stained suits of armor guarded every corner, and long wooden tables stretched across the black and white checkered floor. There was a short line of people standing in front of a low counter where the menu was displayed overhead, pen-written on large leather scrolls. Tacky, trumpet-centric music blasted from the loudspeakers and made the spacious fast-food restaurant feel busier than it actually was.

Leo pulled out the $20 bill that had been burning a hole in his pocket.

“This is the perfect home for him,” Leo said, snapping the money straight.

“I feel like the motel we saw is the type that lets people stay, but doesn’t ever let them leave.”

Boy squinted to read the cursive menu as they moved up a place in line.

“It gave me crime scene vibes. Someone has been or will be murdered there, no question,” Leo added.

When it was their turn to order they approached the counter apprehensively. The teenager at the register was wearing a harlequin hat with two bells on the end and a tee shirt printed with a chainmail design. His official rank was unclear, but the clash of congruity was compensated for by the employee’s unwavering commitment to character.

“Welcome to Burger Palace! How may I be of service to you?”

Leo took a step backwards and Boy put his hands in his pockets.

"Hi. How are you?" Leo asked.

"Every day is a privilege to serve your highness." The employee's voice cracked and he patted his throat. Leo nodded.

"I am Leo, this is Boy."

"Two new kings to the castle, a true honor."

The employee curtsied and eagerly awaited their orders.

"We would like, please, two burger meals," Leo said.

"Ask and you shall receive. Which combination would most please you?"

"Um, the number two meal, please," Leo said.

"Two number twos and you won't have to ask twice, your majesty. Would you like to make the meals royal?"

"What does that mean?"

"Double the meat and cheese, your excellence."

"Yes please, sir."

The employee laughed giddily and gave a deep bow. He punched around on the computer screen and traded their $20 bill for several smaller ones and some coins.

"When your feast is prepared we shall bring it to you chivalrously," he said.

"Where do we sit?" Leo asked.

"Any throne is yours for the taking," he said, giving a shake of his fist.

The boys took their number off of the counter and walked over to a high-top table with round stools sticking out of the floor.

"Hey look, they spin," Leo said, twisting in his chair as he took a seat.

Boy pushed himself back and forth with his foot, disappointed that they didn't spin all the way around. Leo picked up a miniature sword and a shield that had been left behind from a kid's meal.

"It's a little cynical to give children weapons of war with their milk and apple slices, don't you think?" Leo said.

Boy picked up the shield and put it on the end of his finger.

"But then again, babies used to be kings back in the day, and war is war whether you know the whole alphabet or not."

Leo stabbed at Boy who blocked the attack with a quick flick. They had a brief battle of phalanges until the fighting was interrupted by the presentation of their food. Two silver trays were lowered down in front of them and two paper crowns were placed upon their heads. Their regal burgers sat atop a golden bed of fries in great glory, the double cheese melted to perfection across the patties. The enchanting smells of oils and salt wafted seductively into the air. The boys went to fill their empty cups at the machine and mixed all of the sodas, taste testing as they experimented with the flavors. They sat again in their twirling thrones, salivating.

"I haven't even taken the first bite and I am already dreaming about the second," Leo said.

Boy ripped open a handful of ketchup packets and poured a pile in the corner of his tray. He started dipping fries like brushes in paint and Leo sunk his teeth into his burger. Every mouthful was dramatic and sensational, each more unbelievably delicious than the last. With his mouth full of half-chewed beef, Leo waved his burger at Boy.

"This isn't just cheese, Boy, you know what it is?"

Boy shook his head and wiped his lips with the back of his hand.

"This is royal cheese, cheese for kings and nobility. Do you think that just anyone can be welcomed through those sacred doors and be offered royal cheese? Is that what you think?"

Boy shook his head. No, they couldn't.

"That's damn right, your majesty."

They laughed together and toasted their drinks to the high life. The boys continued eating without pause until they were stuffed, and then they ate more. All that was left on their fancy trays were grease stains and discarded sauce packets. They sat back and placed their hands on their stomachs, admiring their work.

"I will never complain about being this full," Leo said, "because I remember being so hungry. All those times we didn't have any food in the fridge of 84 D, I would think about what I would do if I was going to open up my own food joint. It would be the place to be, I promise you that."

Leo took the lid off of his soda and swirled the ice around with his straw.

"I would make it like a breakfast diner, but it would be breakfast at night. Better yet, it would be brunch – brunch at night. Brunch at night in a nightclub. All of the booths would line the walls and in the center would be a disco dance floor, so people could party while they wait for their food. It would be space themed, of course, with planets painted on the walls with neon paint and glow in the dark stars on the ceiling. We will call it Pluto's Plate. On Tuesdays we will have roller skating."

Leo took a long sip of the soda at the bottom of his cup. Boy's eyebrows were raised.

"What? Boy, we *never* had food in that fridge. I have had a lot of time to work out the details."

It was true that there was rarely anything to eat, but the absence of food was never surprising. It was just another one of the many basic human needs that was deficient in their upbringing. There was no denying the quality of life they had lived, but this was a new day. They were wearing crowns inside of a castle, eating until they were full and chose to stop. Where they had been was nothing compared to where they were going. The world was now their kingdom.

One too many soda refills sent Boy searching for the bathroom through the medieval maze of tables and décor. He found the restroom and walked in, passing by a little boy who was struggling to reach the sink to wash his hands. Boy chose the urinal closest to the wall and let out a liter of carbonated pee with a sigh of relief. He flushed with his elbow and then rinsed his hands in the deep metal basin. The small boy was now standing directly under the hand dryer, pushing in the button and letting the air blow onto his face. The boy giggled as he shifted his head and his skin was pushed in different directions. The dryer shut off and the boy stood there for a moment, looked at Boy who was holding his wet hands out in front of him, and then pressed the button again. The boy sent his curly brown hair flying like he was riding a roller coaster. This time when the dryer stopped he approached Boy.

"Can you tie my shoes? I can't remember how," he said.

Boy nodded, wiping his hands on his pants. He dropped to one knee and carefully looped the bunny ears and double knotted the laces. The boy looked at his shoes and smiled, then walked out of the bathroom. Boy wiped his hands on his pants again and made his way for the door but then hesitated. He checked for feet beneath the stalls and glanced at himself in the mirror. Boy slapped the button and stuck his head under the dryer until it shut off. Then he hit it again.

When Boy rejoined Leo at the table he had a paper bag full of food sitting in front of him. He was pulling a French fry out of the top of it.

"They made an announcement that they were closing, so I ordered us another number two to go. I didn't want our money to go to waste."

Boy stuck his head inside the bag and inhaled. It smelled better than wild flowers. It smelled like deep fried roses.

"Either that guy behind the counter is actually from the Middle Ages, or he deserves a raise because he refuses to talk normally," Leo said, grabbing the bag and standing up.

The boys walked to the exit and pushed open the heavy wooden door into a wall of rain. It was torrential, biblical rains that had already flooded the castle's moat. As the restaurant closed behind them the two boys were forced to step outside. They were instantly drenched. The cold drops soaked through their clothes, their skin, and their steaming bag of food. They looked at each other in disheartened disbelief. Boy saw the child from the bathroom climbing into the backseat of his mother's car. Their engine started noiselessly and they drove away. Everyone was gone again. Even the door to the motel across the street had been closed.

Boy and Leo stood helplessly in front of their castle as the night's storm ended their reign. They were heirs to nothing. They had fallen far from their thrones – kings on the inside, peasants on the outside.

They threw their paper crowns in the trash.

Chapter 13: Failure to Launch

There are rare, coincidental times in life where one is lost both figuratively and literally, simultaneously. This was one of those times. The two travelers had lost faith in their direction. The maps had told lies of the river's length. It was like walking on nature's treadmill. With each step to nowhere they felt more and more trapped within the infinite metaphor. To make morale worse, the rains had flooded the river and shaken the trees, littering their endless path with obstructive debris. The bank had narrowed to a tightrope walk along the river's edge. There was no going forward and they swore they would never go back, so they were left without many points on the compass to choose from.

"I was wrong," Leo said.

He tossed his duffle bag on the ground. It had been doused from using it to shield his face from the rain throughout the night. The golden light had returned, but all it did was illuminate the devastation. It was like a rainbow after a hurricane. It was hard to be inspired by the beauty.

"If we were going the right way we would have been there by now, and if we have been going the wrong way the whole time then I have no idea where we are," Leo said.

He grimaced.

"I don't think we are going to make it, Boy. What do you think?"

Boy gave an indecisive shrug.

"That's what I thought."

Leo unzipped his bag, grabbed a handful of his old photographs that he had saved from his box and walked over to the river's lip. Without a final glance he tossed them into the raging water in riddance. The memories were washed away as if the moments were never remembered at all.

"Those were weighing me down," Leo said, throwing his bag back over his shoulder.

"The only solution is to cross the river and continue on the other side. There aren't as many trees over there so we should have room to walk."

Boy glanced at the rushing water of the overflowing river. It had the shape of a deadly serpent slithering between the trees. Its continuous roar was harrowing and hypnotizing. It was not a trap, it was a peril; the danger was poorly disguised. Boy nodded, as ultimately, there was nothing new to be afraid of. Fear had many faces; this was just another one of its expressions.

"If we can hop from one rock to the next we can make it. The water is too deep and moving too fast to try and wade across."

Boy eyed the shimmering tops of the boulders poking just above the water's surface.

"I'll go first," Leo said, stretching one foot out over the river. He quickly lost his balance and returned his foot to the grass on the river's edge. He steadied himself and took a short breath.

"I can't," Leo started, lifting his leg again but then dropping it back to the ground. "I can't see the rocks."

Leo adjusted his glasses and tilted his good eye towards the water. He lined his vision with the rock and aimed his foot at it. The bottom of his shoe landed on the top of the boulder as the water splashed over his leg. Leo stuck his arm behind him to give Boy a thumbs up.

There was promise in Leo's unshakeable confidence, but no matter how bold, bad plans just don't last very long. As soon as Leo trusted his foot on top of the mossy rock it deceived him. He slipped sideways and reached out to brace his fall but there was nothing to grab hold of. He flipped on top of his flailing arm and it was violently wedged between two large rocks. His glasses dove into the river and he let out a bestial scream. Boy grabbed on to Leo's bag, whose strap had wrapped around his chest, and dragged him out of the water. Leo writhed on the ground in pain and Boy saw that his right arm had a new angle. The skin around his forearm was stretched tightly over the break. Leo pushed himself up straight with his legs and placed his back against a tree. His broken arm lay limply at his side.

Boy put his hand over his mouth and walked away from his friend.

"We can fix this," Leo said with little air in his voice.

Boy, who could not well handle the sight of blood, fared worse with the sight of bones. He bent over and vomited on top of a pile of leaves.

"We can fix this," Leo repeated through clenched teeth as he tried to drag his arm closer to his body.

Boy looked back at the escaping bone, pitched like a tent beneath Leo's pale skin. He crouched down, forced himself to swallow, and threw up again. He wiped his lips with the back of his hand and then wiped his hand on the grass.

Leo tried to use his legs to lift himself off of the ground but lost his balance and fell back down on his splintered bone. He let out a guttural cry and tried to hold his arm together with his hand. Leo closed his eyes and took a series of short, uncomfortable breaths. Boy sat with his back to his best friend, unable to help, and incapable of watching him suffer.

"I don't know, Boy, I just don't know."

Boy knew. Boy knew that this is where the river ended. This was as far as they would go, as far as they had ever been, but it would not be far enough. It was the truth, but Boy understood that Leo would never accept it. He would believe in his own truth devotedly until it broke him down slowly. It was self-preservation, for reality's truth would have destroyed him all at once. Leo had focused on his breathing to control the pain. Boy knew he was listening to Leo's dream take its final breaths. Once Leo finished exhaling his dream into the atmosphere, who would be left behind? Boy realized that he had never separated the dream from the dreamer. He only knew his best friend by a destiny that defined him. He feared that Leo and his dream would perish together. Boy had to save him. He had to make Leo's dream come true. Boy had to be a hero.

He closed his eyes and tried to visualize the universe, but it was too big for him to imagine. He tried to define it, set boundaries on the galaxies, but struggled to contain the sea of swirling stars. His imagination was meeting its match – one endlessly expanding entity attempting to enclose the other. Boy needed reinforcements. He looked to Leo. Space would take two minds to imagine.

Leo was shaking and begging for the pain to stop as Boy approached him. Boy couldn't take the pain away, but he could take Leo away from the pain. He could take Leo as far away as one could go. He gently grabbed the resting hand at the end of Leo's broken arm.

The colors drained from Boy and bled into Leo's eyes as the ceiling of the sky lifted to reveal an untouched carpet of darkness. The universe was unscripted. They were going to build a world on top of the world and launch themselves into it. Their rocket awaited them. Boy strapped himself in next to Leo who was testing the range of his no longer broken arm. His face was hidden behind the glass of his helmet, hiding any emotions that he may have been feeling. Boy gave him a pat on the shoulder but Leo didn't react. Boy began to question his decision to drag Leo from reality, but he felt a reassuring tug on his spacesuit from the seat behind him. Elle was fastening herself in and rubbing her gloved hands together excitedly. She pointed to the sky with a sly wink. Boy gave her a salute. She needed to be there, Boy told himself. She wouldn't have missed it for the world.

The countdown began and Leo folded his hands in his lap and stared straight ahead. Boy prepared to clear his mind to allow it to see whatever it may see. He stole a glance at Leo and saw that his lips were trembling. When there were no more numbers left to count Boy launched them into the final frontier of his fantasy. Instantly, rightfully, they became the center of the universe, drifting through as the celestial bodies orbited around them. They were in the museum of the mind's outermost limits and the artwork was extraordinary.

Vortexes weaved intricate luminescent webs between painted planets dripping with color as cotton candy galaxies were scattered by burning honeycomb comets. Their surging rocket soared through clusters of stars, tornados of light and shattered nebulas of kaleidoscopic crystals. They witnessed the revolutions of soap bubble moons and collisions between married marbles adorned with heavenly rings. They cut through jellyfish clouds of cosmic dust and paused by a pulsar the shape of a beating heart.

Leo's mouth hung slightly open as he marveled at the universe. He had made it to space and it was not as far away as he thought it would be.

Leo put his hand on the glass in front of him and pointed at the astronaut floating patiently in the distance. He looked to Boy uncertainly, almost fearfully.

"How long has he been waiting for me?"

Boy gave Leo a gentle push out of the ship and he ejected into the open space. Leo drifted towards his waiting father and revolved around him slowly. They floated face to face, but kept space between them. Leo awaited his father's embrace. When Boy decided that they had orbited long enough, Leo's father reached out and pulled his son close to him. Their love became their gravity.

"You are a hero, Boy," Elle said, leaning over his shoulder to watch the interstellar reunion.

"You saved his world."

Elle kissed the side of his helmet.

Boy felt weightless. He thought back to the day that his story started, the day they took his mother from him and left him to author the tale on his own. It was the worst day of his life. This would be the best day of his life.

Boy watched Leo and his father drift through their imagined universe side by side.

He wanted to let them float in his fantasy for an eternity, but even forever wouldn't have been long enough. It was time to bring them back down to Earth. There would be no supernova ending. There would be no big bang. Boy slowly pulled the stars back into the darkness, one by one, as if he were turning off the lights.

***

"Why did you do that?"

Once Boy's colors drained from Leo's eyes they looked empty.

"Why would you do that to me?"

Boy let go of Leo's hand and backed away from him.

"What do I have left now?"

Boy wiped away the colors that were falling from his eyes. The tinted drops stained his cheeks as they crawled to his chin.

"So, that was it? That was my life?"

Leo moaned as he leaned his weight on his crooked arm. He shifted his body against the trunk of the tree, pressing the side of his head against the bark.

"What a joke."

Leo stared at Boy, but it was as if he didn't see him at all.

Boy pulled the bandana off of his head and felt betrayed. The boy with the bandana was supposed to be a hero. That was how the story was meant to be written, but Boy had become the villain. He had stolen a dream and trapped it inside of his fantasy. The bandana in his hands was cursed. He wished it had burned in the fire in 84 D. Now it would haunt him forever and it wasn't even his bandana.

"Could you give me a minute, Boy?"

Boy wanted to give his best friend everything he ever wanted, but he did not want to give him a minute. He did not want to leave his side. He wanted to protect him, but it was clear that he couldn't. He was hurting him. He had not saved him and now he never would. Boy, too, needed a minute to digest that truth. He crumpled the bandana and shoved it to the bottom of his backpack before he stood and sulked away. When he reached the top of the river bank he took a long look back at Leo, who was watching the water sedately. Boy tried to imagine his friend far away from that river and far away from outer space, but he couldn't imagine exactly where that would be.

As Boy broke through the clearing he found himself on the outskirts of a suburban neighborhood. He stood at the end of an empty cul-de-sac next to a basketball hoop held down at its base by bags of garden mulch. There was a ball sitting on the grass next to his feet. Boy scanned the block before scooping the ball up under his arm and walking onto the asphalt. He turned the ball over in his hands and gave it a squeeze. He dropped the ball and let it bounce back up to him.

Boy could not believe how quickly he had fallen. He had not only given Leo a new world to live in with his father, he had given him an entire galaxy, a universe of his colors, but the pain had patiently awaited their return.

Boy gave the ball a dribble and then another. He lifted it above his shoulders and shot it towards the hoop. It hit the front of the rim and rolled back to him.

Leo's dream was dead and Boy could not resuscitate it. That much Boy had accepted.

He picked up the ball and shot it again, this time slightly higher. The ball hit the backboard and caromed away from him.

If there was any hope left alive of Boy becoming a hero, Leo needed a new dream, a dream that he believed in and that Boy could help him actualize.

He collected the ball that had come to a stop against the curb and walked it over to the front of the hoop.

Boy could not live out his dream if Leo did not live out one of his own.

Boy reached up and tossed the ball over the front of the rim and it slid down through the net.

Their adventure would have to carry on and it no longer mattered in which direction.

Boy left the bouncing ball behind him and made his way back to Leo. He eased his way down the bank, holding on to tree branches to avoid slipping on the layer of mud and wet leaves that covered the ground. As he broke into the clearing he was welcomed by the golden light that lit their hidden stage. It was such a delicate glow, spotlighting Boy from above as he approached the river's edge. It was deceitful, however, for Boy no longer shared the stage. Leo was gone. Alone by the rushing water, in front of an audience of none, Leo had played out his final act. Boy knew there would be no encore.

Leo's bag lay abandoned in the shade of a tree. Boy looked to the left, then to the right, and to his left again as if he were crossing a busy intersection. He stuffed his hands in his pockets, dropped his head to his chest and then dropped to his knees. Boy watched the river run away from him. He did not give chase.

Boy reached into his backpack and dumped his journal and his bandana into the wet grass at the edge of the river. He folded the bandana on his lap and wrapped it around the face of the journal. Boy tied the two ends together and knotted it tightly. It was time to drown his dream. Boy wanted it to die the same way it had killed his best friend.

That's what Boy wanted, but he couldn't do it.

He let himself fall onto his back with his arms spread out at his sides; his legs were folded sideways on top of each other. He lay on a pile of fallen sticks from the shaken trees. Their sharp points pierced his skin. The heavenly light draped his body in gold as a red drop slipped from the corner of his eye.

His colors were to be sacrificed. His hero's journey was far from over.

Boy rose again.

Leo had been left in outer spacc to explore with his father. That is where he was and where he would remain. That is what Boy told himself as he turned his back on the river that he had followed far enough. He climbed up the bank and looked out from the fringes of suburbia. He walked past the restless basketball and came to a stop in the middle of the street. The sun was shining as if no one was suffering, but Boy needed to find someone else to save. Since he knew no one, it could be anyone, and since it could be anyone, he could go anywhere. Mr. Man had shown him that the best way to find someone was to lose himself. So, with his bandana tied around his journal like a bow on a gift, or a noose on a neck, Boy decided to wander until he was lost for good.

Chapter 14: Backseat Drivers

The soft sound of the radio faded in and out as the signal was scattered amongst the towering pine trees that lined the sides of the paved road. A small dangling cross vibrated against the rearview mirror as the rattling truck weaved along the snaking asphalt and the headlights bleakly lit the way through the night. A leathery weathered hand reached across and adjusted the radio dial, small twist after small twist, until a hushed voice began to preach clearly through the speakers. The old hand turned up the volume and then placed itself properly back on the wheel.

"I want to talk to you today about *miracles.* Firstly, let it be known that we ourselves are miraculous in our own existences. We are the living proof of divine intervention, for not only are we created from miracles, we were gifted the capacity to create miracles of our own – which in and of itself is miraculous. However, this message today is not a call to action, but rather a call to attention. We have shown a propensity towards resentment, a tendency to feel abandoned or betrayed if our prayers are ignored or our questions are left unanswered. We have deceived ourselves with our own deception; we have not been forgotten, we have been negligent. We have been oblivious to the everyday miracles, the *ordinary* miracles that are anything but ordinary – those which we don't perceive as miraculous because our hearts and our minds are not vigilant, not perceptive to the truth that every act is a benediction. The answers to all of our questions were born with us, long before we knew what we did not know. No longer shall we hold open palms and beg for miracles, for it is time to wrap our fingers closed around the miracles that exist in front of us, or put those idle hands to work and create miracles for ourselves. We must use the gift that was bestowed upon us. We cannot sleep through our lives and stagger through the obscurity. We must gather around the light. We must wake an entire nation of sleeping beings. We must wake up."

The radio scratched to static and Boy dug his dirty fingernails into his eyelids to hold them open. His bloodshot eyes twitched from side to side as he tried to fight the fatigue and the comfort of dreaming that was pulling him in. Boy stretched the seatbelt off of his chest from where he sat in the center of the backseat and tried to use the strap to brace his head. Boy stared straight ahead and watched the white lines of the road disappear beneath the truck and replace themselves again. Soon, the mesmerizing motion of the vehicle placed the sleep-deprived boy in a trance and he could no longer resist the temptation.

The click of the seatbelt next to him forced Boy's eyes open again. Posturing next to him, grooming himself to his faint reflection in the window, carefully laying each obedient strand of hair in its designated place, was Mr. Man. Boy shook his head and tried to blink him away but Mr. Man was already buckled in for the ride.

"When you blur the line between your fantasy and your reality, it becomes difficult to distinguish which side of the line you are on."

Boy reached a curious hand towards the living, breathing figment of his imagination.

"Breaking every bone in your body, one after another in descending order from largest to smallest, would be far less torturous than the pain I would inflict upon you if you were to place that filthy hand on one of my pinstripes."

Mr. Man had been haunting Boy. He was a leaky faucet of thought that dripped continuously into Boy's consciousness. Mr. Man visited his mind often when times were darkest, always overstaying his welcome. Boy had been homeless, struggling to survive on the unforgiving streets as he searched for someone to save. He had hit rock bottom and Mr. Man had awaited his arrival.

Mr. Man patted down his suit and coolly folded one leg over the other. He scanned Boy's disheveled appearance with scathing contempt.

"If in my worst nightmare I were to go through what you have just gone through, I would most likely never sleep again. You have, indirectly, murdered your best friend in a pathetic and irresponsible attempt to be something you are not."

Boy fidgeted uncomfortably in his seat, casting his twitching eyes down to his feet as he relived and tried to rearrange the sequence of events.

"That is not what happened. How dare you imagine yourself to be courageous! It is perjury to manipulate a memory," Mr. Man snapped, grasping Boy's chin sternly and then flicking it away and wiping his hand on the seat.

"The audacity you must possess to try and tamper with the evidence when I have seen the whole tragedy play through your mind over and over again. What happened that day was predictable and avoidable, and now look at you, already just a stain of what you once were."

Boy glanced self-consciously at the dried spots of color on the neck of his white tee shirt. Mr. Man cocked his head sideways and his colorful eyes spun slowly as he spoke.

"I can see it now. You and the half-blind fool sneak off into the night like a pair of bootleg criminals. You thought you were fleeing to freedom, until you realized that a true prison has little to do with iron bars. You may not be locked away but you are serving a life sentence, as was he. You knew he wouldn't ever go back to that home, he promised you, and he kept his promise didn't he?"

Boy squeezed his hands together in his lap.

"You tortured that poor boy with your utopian illusions. You tried to give him what you thought he needed, but you ended up taking it from him. That was selfish. You offered him a perfect fantasy to fix an imperfect reality. It is almost beautiful, in a pathetic way, you imagining them together, floating in space, but it was not yours to imagine. If you really cared for that boy you would have never encouraged him to chase his dream. You would have taught him that there are only nightmares. This you should be well aware of by now, since you have been living in one your entire life."

Mr. Man pointed a finger at the peaceful old man in the front seat.

"This poor, unsuspecting future victim of yours, the round man driving the truck, nauseatingly I might add, is the man who scraped you off of the sidewalk where you were living like a kicked rat. He wants to give you a home and a family, but you aren't worthy of either."

Mr. Man's voice hushed but intensified. "How many nights did you sleep alone on those streets? How many people spat on you, not with their mouths, but with the disgust in their eyes? I saw you eat out of that garbage, you animal. You could have feasted in your own world and you deserved to starve in this one. You were searching for someone to save? Who did you find?"

Mr. Man balled his hand into a fist and opened it slowly to show Boy his empty palm, emphasizing that Boy had found nothing.

"I don't know what your plan is. I am assuming you don't have one at all, but if you are going to try and 'save' this man here you might as well spare him the time and trouble now by grabbing the steering wheel and spinning us into one of those trees."

Mr. Man leaned back in his seat and looked out the window, tapping his knuckle steadily on the glass.

"Even living inside of your mind I find it hard to fathom what you expected to happen. You thought you could borrow a father? Why would he love you? Why would he let you love him? You are a walking tragedy. I will take none of the blame for this. You should have listened to me when I spoke. You should have let yourself fall off the cliff, but here you are clinging on for dear life. You should have never listened to that shoestring girl with the tacky purple dress."

The seatbelt on Boy's left snapped into place and a familiar voice snatched their attention.

"My name is Elle Lavender."

Elle placed a hand on Boy's shoulder and leaned around him to confront Mr. Man, who had slid himself closer to the door.

"*This* is who I am," she said with a wave at her dress, "but you, you could have been anyone, and *that* is who you chose to be?"

Elle's eyes violated him from top to bottom.

"Very unoriginal."

Mr. Man clenched his teeth but continued in a softer tone, "As I was saying, before we were rudely interrupted, you should have kept yourself safe inside of a world that you could control."

"You want him to hide?" Elle asked.

"I want him to make better decisions."

"What decision would that be?"

"Escape."

"Escape?"

"Yes. You see, to escape is a choice, a choice that we all have, a choice that we make every single day. Look around you. Look at the wandering people with their absent eyes. All you see are bodies, lifelessly commuting to the moments of their lives, but one must ask, where are their minds? Wherever they may go, it is to a far more perfect place than that from which they are leaving. Imagine an existence without limits. Imagine the creations that human hands could never construct. Imagine living in a world custom crafted for your every pleasure. My point should be very clear: no one would willingly choose the life that they live over the life they live in their minds. Boy has suffered enough out there."

"I wouldn't. I would choose the real world," Elle challenged.

"Then you my dear, simply lack imagination."

Mr. Man pulled the knot tighter on his tie.

Elle didn't respond, but rolled down her window to let in the cool breeze from the night.

"Why are you here?" Elle asked.

"Why are you here?"

"Because I love Boy."

Boy turned his head to Elle.

"You and your ideas are hurting him."

Boy turned his head to Mr. Man.

"There is nothing wrong with pain," Elle said.

Boy turned his head back to Elle.

Mr. Man adjusted his seatbelt and shifted uncomfortably.

"Are you even aware of the magnitude of the gift that he possesses?" Mr. Man asked.

"It is a gift to share if he wishes," Elle said.

"It is a gift to keep. I don't understand how you support this prostitution of his mind."

"I will always prefer reality," Elle said.

"Yet you love to escape with him, you love when he gives you a world all for yourself. Hypocrite."

"You do not live where you vacation." Elle's voice tensed.

Mr. Man directed his words at Boy. "You don't owe anything to anyone."

"He owes it to himself."

"Well, then he will be the one to pay the price."

"Let him finish his story," Elle barked.

"That is not his story. He is not the one holding the pen out there," Mr. Man roared back.

"Let him speak for himself."

"These are his words."

Elle cracked her knuckles and patted down her dress violently.

"How can you be so idealistic?" Mr. Man asked, shaking his head.

"Look at the lives you have lived; how much more can you possibly endure?"

"As much as I need to," Elle said coldly.

"You enjoy the torture?"

"I love the life that I have lived." Elle's voice quivered with force.

"Well, Boy does not love his, so you do not speak for the both of you."

"Just because you gave up on everything does not mean that we have to."

"There was nothing for me to give up," Mr. Man said sharply.

"Of course there was, you chose to be lonely," Elle said.

"I am not alone."

"You live under a cardboard box."

"I live in a mansion!"

Mr. Man punched the headrest of the seat in front of him.

"That boy was emotionally unstable and you took advantage of him to fulfill your own narcissistic prophecy."

"How dare you."

"He needed help."

"This has nothing to do with you."

"He didn't have to die." Mr. Man's voice surged with rage.

"I didn't want to die…" a weak, apologetic voice interrupted from the front passenger seat.

All eyes turned to Leo, who was soaking wet, blue and shivering, putting on his seatbelt over his shoulder.

"I'm sorry. This wasn't part of the plan," Leo said.

Boy fixated on the drops of water falling from the soaked strands of Leo's hair. It reminded him of the night he watched the rain from the broken window.

The rattling sounds of the truck mixed with the searching radio static in the silence.

"Where do we go from here? This was supposed to be the end," Mr. Man said in an uneasy whisper.

"Well, it can't end like this," Elle said, sticking her arm out of the rolled down window.

Mr. Man took a long, disappointed look at Leo quivering in the front seat, his hands clutching at the goosebumps on his arms.

"It will be a blessing if it ends at all," Mr. Man said.

He unbuckled his seatbelt and gave a slight ceremonious bow to the crowd before opening the door and jumping out. As he made his exit, the truck screeched to a stop and the old man in the front seat turned around with his hand on his chest.

"Is everything okay back there, son?"

Boy was alone, leaning across the seats and holding the back door open with an outstretched arm. He sat up quickly and closed the door, confirming with a nod that he was okay. The man patted the steering wheel, pressed on the gas and slid back onto the road.

"You just hang tight back there, we will be home before you know it," the man said, turning the radio up once again.

Boy looked out of the window at the unfamiliar darkness that surrounded them and doubted that he would be home soon. Boy did not have much faith in miracles.

Chapter 15: Foundations of a Family

The small girl gave Boy a nudge in the ribs with her foot to see if he was dead. She crouched down next to his head and began to probe him with a small twig that had a leaf stabbed through the end of it. The girl then stood and circled curiously around Boy's sprawled out body; his leg was folded unnaturally behind his back and one arm was tucked behind his neck. She walked backwards a few steps to create space between herself and the body, then took one giant lunge forward and drove a kick into his side that landed with a solid thud. Boy let out a gasping cough and rolled himself upright in a dazed confusion. He shook his head as the blurry image of the young girl's face came into focus. The girl who was staring down at him had fair skin and light blue eyes. Her dirty blonde hair was tangled into a messy braid and two buckteeth stuck out from behind her chapped lips. She wore a faded pair of denim overalls over a white long sleeved shirt that failed to cover the full length of her gangling arms. She stood sturdy in a pair of brown, worn work boots.

"Sleeping on the job, huh?" Skyler's high-pitched voice rang out with disapproval as she shoved her hands beneath her armpits and shook her head.

"I saw the whole thing with my own two eyes. You tried to pull a splinter out of your hand there, saw some blood, started to wobble like a bowling pin, and went down like a sack of potatoes." Skyler's excited voice carried a subtle accent from the south.

Boy felt queasy again, remembering the shard of wood lodged into his palm. Skyler grabbed his wrist and pulled his hand towards her face, squinting to get a good look at it.

"Don't move a muscle," she instructed, sticking her tongue out for precision as she squeezed out the splinter. She held up the fragment of wood for Boy to see and then flicked it on the ground.

"Now, if you are done fooling around, Boy," she said, using all of her weight to help pull him to his feet, "we have to finish moving all of this wood to the shed before supper time. If we get in trouble it will be your entire fault."

Boy nodded in agreement and apology, then bent over and picked up two logs of wood from the pile. Skyler grunted and picked up three that were nearly bigger than she was and waddled her way up the path to the house with Boy right behind her.

"Like I was saying before your nap, Nans says I got a temper because I used to get into lots of fights before we moved. They used to kick me out of school all of the time to punish me, which didn't make any sense to me because I liked not being in school. If they wanted me to stop getting into fights they should have made me go to more school. Sometimes adults can be pretty stupid about things. I think Nans likes to exaggerate things too, because I'm only 10 years old and

I have only been in 5 fights, which is not even one a year. So when you think about it, I probably don't have anger management problems."

Skyler was beginning to lose her breath trying to carry the logs and talk at the same time but it didn't deter her storytelling.

"The first fight I ever got into was with Ruby, my sister. You'll meet her soon maybe. So, I don't think that time even really counted because she is family. She cut off my ponytail so I stabbed her with the scissors. It wasn't a fight as you can see, but I did have to talk to a psychologist after. My second fight, if we are counting that first one as a fight – if not then it would be my first fight – my first or second fight was with Jason from math class. It was in the cafeteria. Jason called me pretty so I blew soda out of my nose at him, then he spat in my macaroni and cheese so I threw my tray at him and punched him in the mouth. He started to cry because his tooth came out, which means it was a good punch, but some people say that his tooth was already a little wiggly and that it didn't count. I also got into a fight with Jason's best friend Tyler because we were playing tag at recess and he promised he wouldn't tag me, so I didn't run, but then he did tag me, and everyone was laughing because he tricked me, so I tripped him when he tried to run away, and then I thought he was going to hit me when he got up so I kicked him in the nuts. I've never lost a fight by the way."

Skyler turned to make sure that Boy was listening but as she did she stepped awkwardly and the weight of the logs tipped her to one side and she went down in a violent crash.

"I'm fine!" she called out before Boy could even begin to help her. Skyler jumped quickly back to her feet and brushed herself off. She grimaced as she tried to put her weight on her leg, but when Boy reached down to pick up one of the fallen logs Skyler stopped him abruptly.

"I can do it. You saw me carry them all the way up here, didn't you?"

Boy backed off, and true to her word Skyler finished carrying the load to the shed with a noticeable limp.

"That's basically all of it." She rubbed her shin tenderly. "But yeah I've never actually lost a fight, but maybe I tied in one or two."

The recognizable rattle of the old truck called their attention down the long gravel driveway, and Skyler hurried to greet her grandfather as he pulled in next to the unfinished garage. The old, leather-skinned man stepped down gingerly from the cab of the truck and gave his shirt a good tucking-in. He grabbed his cherry red toolbox from underneath the seat and placed it on the hood of his truck. Skyler wrapped her arms around his waist and gave him a strong hug, nearly knocking them both over. The old man chuckled.

"Hey Pops, you just missed it. I fell carrying a huge pile of the wood and I almost broke my leg. Look!"

Skyler limped around in a circle to demonstrate how serious her injury was and her Pops watched with a grin.

"Well, I'll tell ya what Sky, I ain't no doctor, but if it were broken I could fix it for ya. A couple nails and screws is all you'd need."

Pops let out a belly laugh and gave his shirt another tuck-in for good measure. He was a big man, not tall but wide, with a round face and soft eyes. His hands were marked from years of work and his face was marked from years of worrying about his family. Pops placed one of those worn hands on Boy's shoulder and gave him a wordless salute. He then turned and looked out at the rawness of the land in front of him. There was a long sloping field of green grass that led to a wall of towering trees that served as the natural gate to hundreds of acres of untouched woodlands.

"From the ground up," he said. "We are going to build everything from the ground up."

Pops motioned to the large framework of the home that sat on top of their green hill. Bare, wooden planks composed the majority of the house, as it was less than half-way finished.

"We don't have much right now, but we have our foundation, and that's what matters most when you are building something to last," Pops said.

"That's right," Skyler added from his hip.

"I am sorry that you are seeing the home like this. I didn't expect it all to take so long, but it will be a cozy place by the time it is finished. We appreciate having you here to help us through it." Pops studied Boy's profile as he scanned the land.

"Hey Sky, why don't you tell him what the first room that we built was?"

"The kitchen," she said with a hungry grin.

Just then the back screen door swung open and a large, curly gray haired woman stepped out wearing a dirty apron and banging a wooden spoon on the back of a metal pot.

"You already know what time it is," she hollered and let the door slam behind her.

***

"Dear Lord this is our grace. By your righteousness we believe our lives to be beautiful. The world bore witness to your resurrection, and now we call upon you to guide us through our own. We are seeds. We shall rise from the dirt in which we were planted. We shall be born anew. Forward is the direction. Our hearts will follow our eyes and our eyes will be on you. We will be loyal to your love and gracious for your wrath. We are humbled by our imperfections, as each new breath is redemption. You give us our air. We will reach the horizon of tomorrow by taking our steps today. We walk upon your words. We carry your message. Until our darkness comes we shall stand by your light. In Jesus' name we pray, amen."

Skyler scooped a mountain of mashed potatoes onto her fork and stabbed it through her steak, leaving it skewered like the sword of Excalibur as she took a long, noisy drink of lemonade.

"You know Nans I've been thinking," she said to her grandma with her lips still on her glass. "If you want me to make friends out here you have to give me a little more freedom to explore."

"What makes you think that I want you to make friends?" Nans replied looking up over her slanted glasses.

"I want you focusing on your school work and nothing else," Nans added. Pops gave a nod of agreement. The two grandparents sat side by side at the head of the table.

Skyler lifted the entire steak off of her plate by the end of her fork and took a ravenous bite. "It's summertime, Nans, there ain't no school to focus on."

"Honey, we are all familiar with the grades that you bring home. It would do you good to get a running start," Nans said and then immediately banged her fist on the table.

"And I swear to the heavens if you don't learn to eat proper at my table you will take your food on the floor like a dog, you understand me?"

Skyler let the steak fall from her teeth back onto her plate and pardoned herself with a rapid apology.

Pops gave his wife a calming pat on the forearm and Nans cracked her neck from side to side.

"Hey Pops, the other day I saw some boys down by the quarry jumping in off the ledge. They were doing flips and stuff and asked me if I wanted to jump too but I told them I had to ask permission first." Skyler feigned innocence.

"Are you trying to ask us a question?" Nans interjected with her head tilted.

"Well, I was just wondering, if maybe it would be acceptable, if I was to possibly jump with them the next time?"

"Oh, you was just wondering huh," Nans said.

"You know you don't have to worry about me Nans," Skyler said.

"I don't have to do anything but eat and breathe, but I am going to tell you no because I like telling you no and because you don't know how to take care of yourself," she said.

"But, Nans, I can hold my own out there, I always do," Skyler said.

"You are too young to *always* be doing anything so quiet down."

Skyler sucked her teeth and pushed some peas to the side of her plate.

"And who told you to be going all the way down to the quarry anyways?" Nans asked.

Skyler's face froze as her mind cycled through her best excuses.

"Well you know, Boy and I been working a lot in the woods, to help with the house and everything, and we finished moving all that wood to the shed like you asked us to. We had no problem getting that done for you, but on one of the trips back and forth I must have got turned around and went the wrong way and got lost."

Nans pulled off her glasses and placed them on the table gently and squeezed the bridge of her nose.

"You got lost?"

"Yes Mam," Skyler gambled.

Boy didn't dare to look up from his plate.

Nans pushed her chair away from the table and threw the napkin from her lap.

"Oh, you wanna play with me. How about I lose this foot up your ass and see if we find it by that quarry?"

"The Lord is listening," Pops chimed in as he touched the cross on his neck and pointed to the printed bible verses that crowded the windows. There were so many holy quotes hung across the panes of glass that barely any light entered the home from outside.

"Well then make sure to tell him that this little girl is testing my holiness," Nans said with finality, pulling her seat back up to the table.

Sky turned to Boy with a wide grin and gave him a playful nudge with her elbow, but Boy ignored her for his own safety.

This was still Boy's first week living with the Johnson family but he had already adjusted to his new life's routine. He and Skyler spent the long summer days doing physical labor around the house and spent their nights saying grace and listening to Nans lose her cool at the dinner table. Boy was not completely sure what he was doing there, in that strange world of relative normalcy that he had only ever watched through windows, but he had stumbled into a family. Although he did not see how this new home played into the rest of his story, the truth was, that for the moment, he was okay with not trying to figure it out. It may not have been heroic, but it was gratifying and safe. Sitting at that table and not hiding in his mind, it seemed that he may have found temporary peace – temporary, because he had not yet been introduced to Ruby.

But then, there she was. Standing in the doorway with her fists clenched, her foot stomped into the floorboard, her nostrils flared, her eyeliner smeared, the bottom of her tee shirt twisted around her skinny waist, the veins popping out of her neck as she screamed at the top of her lungs, is how Boy met Ruby. She turned and slammed the door closed with two hands and then a foot, threw her phone down a side hallway, stormed to the table, and flung herself down into a chair across the table from Boy all while continuing to scream. When she finally ran out of breath she threw her arms across her chest, sank into her seat and stared menacingly at Boy.

It was obvious enough to say that Ruby had an aggressive aura, but it was extenuated by her intimidating appearance. Her look was messy and reckless, as was her attitude. She had striking sapphire eyes, big, softly bruised lips that teasingly hid a pair of slightly gapped teeth, boldly arching eyebrows and a small silver ring pierced through her nose that split her face with perfect symmetry. Her messy blonde hair was pushed sloppily to one side of her head, exposing a long, slender neck.

"What the hell are you staring at?"

That is how Ruby met Boy.

"Who the hell is he?" Ruby upturned an incredulous hand.

"Please don't use that language at the dinner table," Pops said, continuing to eat his meal.

"That's Boy," said Skyler while squishing the brains out of a pea with her fingers.

"Shut up creature," Ruby snapped and turned back to her grandparents for an explanation.

"Ruby don't talk to your sister like that…and Skyler so help me God if you don't change the way you eat *I* will change the way you eat."

"I hate it here," Ruby said crossly.

"Why *are* you here?" Skyler mumbled.

"What happened to living with Tyler?" Nans asked.

"I don't want to talk about it," Ruby rejected.

"To be honest we don't really care but we know we are going to hear about it whether we want to or not," Nans amended.

Ruby pursed her lips and dug her fingernails into her arms.

"He told a joke so stupid that I had to break up with him," Ruby said.

"You broke up with him over a joke?" Nans asked.

"A bad joke."

"How bad was it?"

"You think I'm being dramatic."

"I know you are being dramatic."

"It was that bad."

"What was the joke?"

"I don't want to repeat it."

"Well, we want to hear it."

"No."

"Make us laugh," Nans crossed her arms tightly across her chest.

"It won't make you laugh because it isn't funny. That's the whole point."

"Well I am already not laughing, so what's the worst that can happen?"

"I don't even remember the whole joke. I didn't even want to hear it in the first place."

"Unless you have a better joke I suggest telling it like he told it."

"This family, that's the joke."

Nans unfolded her arms and reached back, grabbing the wooden spoon off the edge of the counter.

"I think you should stick to telling other people's bad jokes."

Ruby quickly understood her options.

"It was a joke about a man with no arms who rang a bell," she started and then stopped, shaking her head with an annoyed sigh.

"You might want to hurry up, I am starting to lose my sense of humor," Nans said.

Ruby stamped her foot in a miniature tantrum and then rapidly proceeded through the joke. "The man with no arms is looking for a job and hears that the church needs someone to ring their bell in the mornings. The bell is at the top of a tower above the church and the pastor doesn't think that he can do it. The man with no arms promises to find a way so the church hires him…How many details do you want because it is a long joke?"

"Every last one," Nans said, tapping the wooden spoon on her forearm with each word.

"His first day on the job he kicks the bell but it hurts his foot, so the second day he uses his hip but it doesn't ring loud enough. The third day he tries to use his back to move the bell but it swings and knocks him over. The pastor sees him struggling and asks him if he is sure he can handle the job and the man says that he can and that he has an idea. The next day the man with no bell…ugh, sorry, I mean the man with no arms uses his head to ring the bell and it works. The man is happy he can make a living, until one day a storm hits the village and the man with no arms gets trapped at the top of the tower. The winds blow the bell and it knocks the man with no arms over the edge and he dies when he hits the ground. The police show up and find the man with no arms dead in front of the church. They ask around for help identifying him because he doesn't have any family in the village. The police stop one of the locals and ask if he knows the man with no arms. The villager looks at the man with no arms, shakes his head and says, 'I don't know his name, but his face rings a bell.'"

Ruby delivered the final line with a straight face and a clenched jaw. The table sat in pensive silence.

"It could have been funny if you told it better," Nans commented.

"There is no funny way to tell a joke that isn't funny," Ruby argued.

"That was a stupid joke," Skyler said with her fork tucked between her knuckles.

"It's not even my joke!" Ruby half-screamed, half-cried.

"Watch your damn tone," Nans threatened.

"Language," Pops reminded.

Ruby stood up in a rage, kicking aside her chair. "I will not be here long," she promised, one defiant word at a time, and stomped her way to her room. Boy watched her walk away through the gaps in the boards of their unfinished walls.

Nans stood at the end of the table and applauded Ruby's performance and then instructed Skyler to start clearing the table and washing the dishes.

"If I cook it, they clean it," she sung in a tune to Boy, plopping back down and waving the wooden spoon like a conductor's baton.

"I thought the joke was pretty clever," Pops chimed in.

"Yeah, it wasn't actually that bad," Nans said with a laugh.

Boy handed off his dirty plate to Skyler with a nod and she balanced it on top of the others on her way to the sink. Nans gave her a warning glare of caution before turning her attention to Boy who sat alone, hunched in his seat.

"This is an adjustment period for the whole family. I think everyone is struggling in their own way with the transition. Ruby has been taking everything pretty personally so we are trying to be patient with her," Pops said.

"Trying," Nans emphasized, holding up the wooden spoon as evidence.

Nans looked over her shoulder at Skyler and lowered her voice.

"We lost their brother in an accident not too long ago," she said.

"May he rest in peace," Pops added.

Skyler banged the dishes around in the sink, drawing a quick glance from Nans.

"We found ourselves in some dark times, so we opened our hearts to the Lord, found our strength in religion, and found you," Nans continued.

"It's miraculous, truly miraculous. The girls had just lost a brother and then the Lord gave you to us, placed you in our path on our way to a new life. Pops was following us out here, needed to pick up some things along the way, and ended up with you in the back of his truck. It's a sign, I swear it."

"A divine sign. I knew that the Lord wanted me to find you. I thought it was a little foolish, picking up a stranger off the side of the road, but what would Jesus have done? God is intentional, it was no coincidence," Pops added, tapping a finger on the table.

"This is all really new to us. All this believing and having faith hasn't been easy. There have been a lot of changes, but these girls are fighters, just like their grandma. I have been fighting my whole life. I've fought to get by, I've fought for love, and I've fought for equality. I haven't put my hands down since I first put them up. There are only two ways that it can really go. Life can either beat you down or toughen you up, and I'm strong. Real strong."

Nans faltered.

"But losing that boy is about the hardest hit I've ever taken."

Over Nans' shoulder Skyler scrubbed the plates with a reckless speed, tossing them from side to side.

"You keep that down now, you can see we are trying to have a conversation," Nans said instinctively, the muscles in her hand twitching. She pulled her glasses back down to the end of her nose.

"His death changed our whole world down there so we came out west to build a new one. I can promise you one thing: this family is going to keep fighting."

The sound of a glass shattering in the sink demanded Nans' full attention once and for all, and she stood quickly with her wooden spoon in hand.

"Boy, you may be excused," she said calmly as Skyler shut off the running water.

"If you want me to give that shirt a wash for you I got a load going in tonight, but it might take a few washes to get those stains out. They look pretty deep."

Boy shook his head no, thank you, and grabbed his backpack that lay by the door and exited out to the front porch. He sat himself on the cushioned swing that faced out to the distant main road and pulled out his journal and laid it next to him. Boy rocked in silence and a steady wind blew open the unclasped notebook. He watched the pages flutter in the breeze. Every life he had lived was captured within that sacred pen and paper, each page scarred with healing ink that bled through the black lines, clotting reality with fantasy for so many years. But there were only a few empty spaces left to fill.

Boy placed his face in his hands and took a breath of the fresh night air but suddenly there was no air to breathe. In that moment it hit him once more that his best friend was dead and he wasn't coming back. The permanency was suffocating. The torture of Boy's life had been endurable knowing that one day it may end, but death left Boy longing for a pain that had come and gone before he had a chance to truly suffer. There was no closure.

Boy pulled out the balled-up bandana that he had buried in his backpack the day he was scooped up off of the side of the road. He pulled on the ends of the cloth and imagined himself ripping it apart. Boy missed his mother. Boy needed his mother. Boy was just a boy, and all boys need their mothers.

Boy lifted his head at the sound of small, unsteady footsteps making their way across the wooden porch. Skyler sat herself next to him, easing herself down gently, her face wincing in pain. She sat on her hands to try and give herself extra cushioning, but she couldn't seem to sit comfortably.

Skyler looked up at Boy and gave him a fake smile. "It only hurts if you let it."

Boy thought of all of the colors on his collar that he had bled, the stains now more vibrant than the colors that remained in his eyes, and nodded in agreement.

It only hurts if you let it.

Boy stared at the sky.

"I really like the stars here, even though I know they are the same stars from back home. Here you can see them better," Skyler said, scooching herself just a tiny bit closer to Boy.

"It is kind of nice having you here with us, Boy. I'm glad Pops found you on the side of the road."

Skyler lifted her feet up and let Boy push them back and forth on the swing.

"How did you end up on the side of the road?" Skyler asked.

That was a good question, but there was no good answer.

Skyler moved herself closer to Boy once more and rested her cheek on his shoulder. Boy looked down and had a revelation; maybe his hopes to become a hero were not completely gone. He knew that soon someone would find him and drag him back to where he escaped from and his adventure would be over. But maybe, just maybe, his final pages would be filled when they did.

Chapter 16: Numbness Beneath the Surface

"You don't have to believe me, Boy. I can tell you don't believe me but it's true. I've never cried in my entire life, except maybe when I was a baby, but there are no pictures of me crying so there is no proof. I didn't cry when Ruby sold my bike or when she broke my finger – she just grabbed it and broke it. I don't know how she did it but I didn't cry. I don't cry when I watch sad movies. I don't cry when my allergies are really bad, or when I eat jalapeños. I never laugh so hard that I cry, even when I think something is really funny."

Skyler balanced herself atop the beat-up metal ladder as Boy held the base from below. Pops was standing at the crest of the hill with his hands clasped behind his back, watching over the woodwork of his newly constructed shed. Skyler had pleadingly convinced her grandfather to let her finish hammering in all of the nails, but it seemed that she was doing more storytelling than manual labor.

The sun was scorching with not a cloud in sight to block its rays, and whether or not Skyler had cried before seemed drastically less interesting while Boy was on the verge of disintegrating. As the merciless sun burned Skyler and Boy as they worked, it tanned the oiled and exposed skin of Ruby, who lay basking on a towel in the middle of the yard. She wore a pair of faded jean shorts that were unbuttoned at the top and rolled down her thighs, with a black tank top that was pushed up beneath her small breasts with the straps slung off of her angled shoulders. White, squared sunglasses covered nearly her entire face and her head rocked back and forth to the music playing from the headphones laid loosely in her ears. Boy wiped at the sweat that fell between forbidden glances at Ruby's bare body.

"Some people say they saw me cry when I wrestled Grayson at the playground. He twisted my arm behind my back and I got dirt in my eye because he shoved my face into the ground, so it was really watery but I wasn't crying. It's not the same thing."

Skyler raised the hammer and aimed at the nail.

"Besides, he cheated because he tackled me when I was tying my shoe. Everyone knows you just don't do that."

She swung the hammer and the head glanced off of the nail and onto her outstretched finger beside it.

"Freak!" Skyler cursed, dropping the hammer and clutching her hand.

"Watch your mouth," Pops called from across the lawn.

"I said freak," Skyler's voice wobbled. She bit down into her bottom lip and tried to shake away the pain. Boy wondered if she was going to cry, but, true to her story, she didn't. She climbed down the ladder slowly and showed Boy her hand. Her fingernail had exploded as if a firecracker had been wedged beneath it. Boy turned away from the sight of the blood and Skyler sulked off towards the house. Pops went to check on her and she waved him off to handle it herself.

"Ruby, go take over for your sister," Pops instructed.

Ruby pretended not to hear him.

"Unless you want to start paying rent," he added.

Ruby sucked her teeth and shut off her music, dropping her glasses and headphones onto her towel. Boy's hands closed tighter around the legs of the ladder as the legs of Ruby strolled seductively towards him. She placed her foot on the bottom rung and tilted her head back to tie up her hair. As she arched her body Boy's eyes fixated on two interweaving beads of sweat that raced down her long, flat stomach, over her ribs and were funneled by her hips, crossing the finish line at her waist where she had neglected to re-button her shorts.

"Don't let me fall," Ruby whispered sarcastically, pushing the words provocatively towards Boy's neck.

Ruby's hands moved swiftly and craftily as she worked, leaning and balancing effortlessly from side to side. Boy was mesmerized by the fluidity of her movements and intrigued by the idea that someone so explosive could exhibit such elegance. Boy could not take his eyes off of her and if he had to be honest, he wasn't exactly trying. Ruby could feel his watching and stopped what she was doing. She climbed backwards down the ladder and then nodded to Boy.

"I want to see you do it."

Ruby put her foot on the bottom rung of the ladder.

"I won't let you fall." She tapped Boy on the elbow and ushered him up.

Boy climbed up the ladder without trusting his feet, tentatively stepping from rung to rung and leaned his full weight against the shed when he reached the top. He picked up the hammer like it was a loaded gun, cautious but curious to see what he could do with it. He pinched the head of a nail between his fingers and pushed the tip into the wood. Boy lined up his sights and lifted the hammer but the nail slipped from his fingers and rolled off of the roof. His knees buckled and he braced himself clumsily as he watched the nail fall into the grass. Ruby walked over to the fallen nail and hovered impatiently above it.

"Pick it up," she ordered.

Boy dropped his head and climbed shamefully down the ladder. Ruby snatched the hammer that he held limply in his hand.

"You are pathetic," Ruby said, shoving the hammer back into Boy's chest. He refused to grab it and it fell to the ground.

"Who do you think you are? You aren't one of us."

Ruby picked up the fallen hammer and held it against his throat.

"You think you can just replace our brother? You could never."

Boy stuck his hands in his pocket and leaned away from the outstretched hammer. His defenselessness infuriated Ruby.

"Say something. You are useless. You are just as dead as him."

Ruby's instant regret softened her face as she lowered the hammer. Boy's eyes shot towards the ground.

It was so easy to hate him.

Boy gave Ruby a weak smile and tried to turn and walk away but she grabbed him by the shoulder.

"Stop, stop, I'm sorry."

Ruby's sharp sapphire eyes had melted into pools of apologetic blue.

"You didn't deserve that," Ruby said, shaking her head vigorously. "I deserved that," she said quietly.

Ruby pulled Boy back over to the ladder and climbed up it again.

"Don't let me fall, please."

Ruby finished hammering in the remaining nails into the loose boards and Boy held the ladder as still as he could. When she climbed back down, Boy offered her his hand and she took it, gently stepping to the ground and avoiding eye contact.

"My hero," she said beneath her breath.

Ruby tossed the hammer to the grass and walked away while buttoning up her shorts.

***

Boy's journal lay next to him on the porch swing, left open and neglected like a careless lover. His attention was on the stars. His eyes traced his own constellations and searched for the secrets that connected them. Whenever Boy was beneath the stars he was reminded of a special night he had shared with Elle. Of course they were all special, but this one in particular was close to his heart.

They were lying on the floor of their room on their backs, side by side, with their arms crossed across their chests. Leo was already asleep in his race car bed. Elle was whispering to herself about how long it had been since she had gazed at the stars and how beautiful she thought it was that the stars were for everyone to share. Staring at the blank ceiling, separated from the sky, Boy wanted to offer her the stars of his mind, but when he reached out his hand she rejected it.

"We will give the stars a night off," was her reason.

"It can't be easy being a star. There must be a lot of pressure on you, with the whole world watching you."

Elle gently ran her nails along her forearms.

"I don't know why anyone would want to be like a star. Isn't it vain for a human being to see a star and think, I am like that? We are so far apart for a reason."

Elle rubbed her eyes with the back of her hand.

"It makes for good poetry though."

Elle rolled her head to the side so that she could see Boy's face, which was lined by the light coming through the window.

"I want to say that I am like poetry, that I am a poem, but that would be like calling myself a star."

Boy turned his head towards Elle and she turned her eyes back to the ceiling. She stuck her finger in the air but it went unseen, dipped into the middle of the night's shadow.

"I only know one poem about stars."

Boy turned his head towards the ceiling and Elle turned her eyes back to Boy.

She spoke the words softly and clearly.

"I am the only star shining on a cold winter night,
I am afraid to look down because I am scared of the height,
Why do you believe I can make your dreams come true?
I search for hope even more than you do.
I am alone but you dreamers are not,
You all come and go while I stay in one spot,
I wish I could fall as much as you wish you could reach me,
We are alike, all of you and I,
We wait for a new day so our true selves can hide,
I have dreams too; I wish to be free,
But I live trapped in the sky as you all wish upon me."

Elle finished her poem and rolled her eyes back to the blank ceiling.

"I bet you've never thought about it like that before."

She was right, he had not. But now, as Boy sat on the swing beneath the carpet of stars, he tried not to expect anything of them, or ask anything from them. Boy could only imagine what the life of a star was like. The only thing he knew for sure was that like his own life, that of a star had a beginning and an end and perhaps a bit of destiny in between. It was not their responsibility to make wishes come true.

Skyler walked out across the porch, her small footsteps sending their customary squeaks through the boards, and took her seat next to Boy.

"Do you love nature?" Skyler asked.

The innocence of her intrigue caught Boy off guard. It was a simple question meant to have a simple answer, but Boy's mind had found a way to complicate it. He did not know if he loved nature because he barely knew nature. He did not feel that he deserved to love nature after having neglected her for his entire life. Boy did not want to diminish the concept of love for the convenience of conversation. Yet, Boy ultimately nodded his head. It was not the time to try and sort all of his scattered thoughts.

"I do too," Skyler said.

She tucked her arms inside of a big sweater that she was wearing.

"My brother did. He loved it more than I did. He loved it more than anything. I think I love it because he loved it, but it is really easy to love. My brother's name is Parker, it was Parker… is Parker… I still don't know how I am supposed to say that."

Skyler lifted her legs off of the ground and let Boy's feet push them back and forth.

"He loved watching the sunrise. He would always wake up and drag his blankets up into a tree. Sometimes he would fall back asleep while he was still up there. He was always the first one up and the last one to school, if he decided to go at all. Nans had a really hard time punishing him because he was so sweet. He would apologize and smile and laugh and was so nice to everyone that no one could stay mad at him."

"This was his sweater," she added, pulling it down over her knees.

"He used to call me Sky. I like when people call me Sky," Sky said.

"No one really explained to me why he died. I think it is because I am young and they don't think I would understand. I know it was drugs. I heard them say he took drugs because he was sad. I didn't think he was sad, but I guess he was *too* sad because he took *too* many drugs."

Sky rested her chin on her knees.

"Boy, I have a question."

Boy folded his hands in his lap.

"Is it okay to feel lonely when you miss someone?"

Boy nodded.

"Well, I miss my brother. Am I going to be lonely forever?"

***

"Hey, Boy."

Boy sat with his back against the shed, fanning himself with his hand. His legs were spread out lazily in front of him. Skyler sat next to him in his shadow, slouched, trying to shield herself from the sun. They were going into their fifth hour of painting the shed with the summer sweltering around them. They had taken a pause to re-strategize their painting approach. Skyler had made it very clear that it was not a break and that she did not need to rest. Ruby, who had called Boy, stood just a few feet in front of them with a white bathing towel hanging from her forearm. The baby hairs on her forehead were a collection of out of control curls that had been frizzed from her sweat.

"Do you want to go swimming down at the quarry with me?"

Ruby was not Boy's friend, but she no longer acted like an enemy. She had not been nice to Boy, but she had been sorry. It was strange dynamic they now shared; Ruby had attacked Boy but became vulnerable. The majority of the time Ruby went out of her way to avoid Boy's presence, but every rare now and again she would approach him, share an intimate thought and then walk away. She seemed to love to be a mystery, but she seemed to love the idea of leaving clues even more. Strange was a relative term, given the life that Boy had lived, but he found it strange how pacified and subdued Ruby had been as of late. So, strange as it may or may not have been, there she was, standing almost timidly, with her towel folded neatly over her arm, barefoot, staring at Boy with glazed eyes, inviting him to swim on a hot day. Boy questioned which side of his imagination he was on.

"Can't you see we are working here?" Skyler said from Boy's shadow.

Ruby looked from one worker to the other.

"I had no idea. I didn't think you two were working, because you aren't."

"We are busy."

"You need Boy to help you? You can't do it by yourself?"

"I don't need anyone's help."

"I didn't think you did."

"You know we aren't allowed to go near the quarry," Skyler said, feigning respect for the rules of the house.

"I know that *you* aren't allowed. Besides, it will be safer if I bring Boy."

Ruby's front teeth slipped over her bottom lip when she gave a torpid smile.

"If he doesn't want to come he doesn't have to. I am not on my knees begging."

Both of the sisters turned their head to Boy and waited to see what he would do.

They saw him stand, nod to Skyler, and walk to Ruby's side. Skyler had always made Ruby out to be dangerous, but every adventure needed a bit of danger. This thought convinced Boy to follow Ruby's long strides into the woods, or maybe it was her sundress sticking to her skin and the way she walked from side to side. It was either one or the other. Motivation, like symbolism, could be quite confusing.

There was no real path leading them to the quarry. They seemed to forge it as they went. Ruby said nothing to Boy along the way, apart from mumbling song lyrics beneath her breath. Every now and then Ruby would look back at Boy and laugh to herself about something without sharing the joke. As they broke through the final cluster of trees Boy could feel a sense of panic creeping in. The edge of the quarry snuck up on them and the woods ended abruptly without warning. Boy slowed his steps, but Ruby was ready to walk right off of the ledge, disregarding the closing distance until her toes were wrapped around the rim of the rock. The drop was nauseatingly high and steep, with several jagged points sticking out of the face of the bluff. The landscape was eerily similar to the cliff in Mr. Man's painting. A set of goosebumps crawled across Boy's skin, one chill at a time. He was petrified by the thought of falling and by the feel of Ruby's open hand on his lower back. She pretended to shove him and then grabbed him quickly.

"You scared? You should be." Ruby's face was covered by a goofy smile.

She let her hand slide off of his back and together they looked out over the vast expanse of water and natural beauty. Distant mountains lined the horizon with faded tops as if a divine creator had begun to erase them. It may have been the most beautiful sight Boy had ever seen, in a terrifying, vertiginous sort of way.

"There are only two ways down," Ruby said, holding up three fingers.

"Front flip or cannon ball." Ruby grabbed Boy's hand and he tried to pull away, but she planted her feet and wrestled with him.

"Or, or, or," Ruby said, losing her breath, "we can take the trail to the bottom."

They split apart panting. Ruby's dress had slid off of her shoulder.

"Three options I guess."

Ruby stepped around Boy and reached back for his arm, pulling him behind her. She guided him down a sloping path carved out of the rock that led to a miniature beach of pebbles and stones. There was a slight breeze traveling across the surface of the water that lifted the bottom of her dress as she dipped her feet in the still water. There was a reverberative silence ricocheting between the walls of rock that surrounded them.

What are you doing here? the quarry asked him.

Boy knew it was Ruby's voice, but it didn't feel like her question.

"I guess you could ask me the same thing," Ruby responded to herself.

"I don't have to be here but I am. Actually, I am not here. I'm never anywhere. I am always on my way somewhere else." Ruby's voice was oozing out between her lips like dripping honey.

"I think going somewhere is always more exciting than being somewhere. This is just me passing through on my way."

Ruby spoke with her back to Boy. He traced her outline with his eyes.

"People say I am rebellious."

Ruby slipped the straps off of her shoulders and let her dress fall into a soft pile at her feet.

"They say I am rebellious because I always do what I want, but they only think it is rebellious because what I want to do isn't what they want me to do. If we both wanted me to do the same thing, I would be very well-behaved. I will always do whatever I want to do, because if you aren't doing what you want, then you are doing what you don't want to do, and why would you do that?"

Ruby walked slowly into the water and Boy watched her naked body transform into reflections beneath the surface. She floated on her back and little waves of water splashed onto her pierced, bare nipples.

"I think I am just talking because I know you will listen," Ruby spoke to the sun.

"Most people don't listen. They hear you, but they aren't listening," Ruby rolled her eyes to Boy.

"I can't decide if you are more like a window and I'm looking right through you, or you are a mirror and I am staring at myself."

"The truth is I am pretty high right now," Ruby said lazily.

"I don't care what you think of me. I don't care if you get to know me, but I am not a bad person. It may seem like I have made some bad decisions in my life, but I've never had many good options to choose from. I'm just human after all."

Ruby rolled over and proceeded deeper into the quarry until she was forced to tread.

"Boy, come in the water."

Boy slowly pulled off his shirt and stripped to his boxers without much of a second thought. It was all too serene to deny, all too stimulating. He folded his arms in front of his chest as he waded in. The cold water immediately made him shiver. He stopped once the water was bobbing beneath his chin, but Ruby swam over and grabbed him, pulling him in deeper.

"I have always had trouble with my emotions," she said, wrapping her legs around Boy's waist.

"I wasn't feeling what I wanted so I decided to feel nothing at all. I let myself go numb. Do you know the feeling?"

Ruby's legs slid up around Boy's ribs and squeezed tightly. Boy could feel his body tingling from the shocking cold.

"But then, I got so used to being numb, I didn't know how to feel anything anymore. It scared me, so I begged the world to make me feel something."

Ruby placed her forehead against Boy's.

"Can you feel anything?"

Boy shook his head as his body began to shut itself down. He could no longer feel his legs that were kicking frantically to keep them afloat.

Ruby stuck out her tongue and on the end there was a white tablet. She slammed her lips against Boy's and wrapped their tongues together. Ruby pulled her head away and Boy could feel the tablet dissolving. He tried to spit it out but she covered his mouth with her hand, wrapped her other arm around his shoulders and dragged him beneath the water. Together they sunk to the bottom of the quarry.

Boy could feel the pressure growing in his chest as they descended. Ruby taunted him with bursts of bubbles streaming from her nose, cheerfully wasting the oxygen that Boy was struggling to hold hostage. She was wrapped around him like an octopus, playfully squeezing the life out of him. Boy tried to pry her arms and legs off of him but she refused to release him. Ruby's form softened in front of him as if she was dissolving in the water. Boy's last breath of air escaped him and he knew it was the beginning of the end. He wondered if this was karma's revenge for not saving his best friend. It was his turn to drown.

Then, inexplicably, his muscles loosened, the colors of his eyes began to pull apart like a lava lamp, and he smiled. The next thing he knew they were gasping for breath and laughing above the surface. Ruby fountained water out of her mouth and onto Boy, who was pounding his chest animatedly with his fists. He imagined that he had been close to death, anchored there beneath the surface, but now it felt just the opposite.

So, feeling everything at once after feeling nothing at all, Ruby and Boy floated on their backs, soaking in the reckless spontaneity of their youth and giving purpose to the reminiscent summer sun.

Chapter 17: Storm in the Magic Garden

"Dear Lord, this is our grace. By your righteousness we believe our lives to be beautiful. We thank you for the tides that return to us after leaving us for the sea. We thank you for the seasons that cycle around us. We thank you for your gravity that keeps us grounded. We thank you for the compasses you have placed inside us. We praise you from our home, from the waters we bathe in, and from the skies that we reach for. We know that you have given time incredible powers – the power to turn girls into women and boys into men – but if our time has come, if the day is near, we beg our sins be forgiven but not forgotten. Judge us harshly when this life ends. We will bear no false witness. We welcome your wrath. Until our darkness comes we shall stand by your light. In Jesus' name we pray, amen."

It is said that the weather is the world's emotion; a manifestation of mood, an expression of sentiment through natural forces, the entire spectrum of affections represented by the elements. The mood of the Earth can change the mood of the people, as the sun or the rain can affect and even alter the human experience. Boy had marveled at the unpredictability of the weather once before, but on this night, his mind was enraptured by the power of a storm. The natural world incites no greater envy amongst the human race than with the spectacle and freedom of a storm. The most extreme emotions that ravage the mind and body are expressed in a most grandiose and destructive fashion. How one wishes their anger would split the Earth or their sadness would flood the streets with thrown waves from the ocean. Boy realized that there would be no greater release than the ability to destroy the world around him time and time again, rather than that which was within him which could only be destroyed but once.

Destruction was precisely the worry of the family that lived in the half-built home beneath the hovering storm. The rains and wind had already arrived, fierce and persistent. Yet as he sat at the dinner table with his hands folded in his lap, Boy could feel another storm coming.

"I'm not waiting anymore," Skyler said, stabbing her fork into her piece of chicken.

"You will wait for your sister. She shouldn't be late for dinner," Nans said.

"She shouldn't, but she always is," Skyler said crossing her arms, leaving her fork plunged into the chicken breast.

The lights flickered and the shutters slammed against the outside of the home. Every few seconds the sky would illuminate and a bolt of lightning would send a flash through the window, highlighting the printed words of the Lord that hung in the frame. Nans looked nervously at the front door, waiting for it to open.

"Are you sure our house can handle this kind of weather?" Nans asked Pops, rolling her hand over her knuckles.

"There are no trees close enough to fall on us, and unless the wind blows us over completely we should be fine," Pops said with his customary calmness.

A strong gale collided with the broad side of the house and the kitchen table rattled violently.

"Should be," Nans repeated.

Just then Ruby stumbled into the house soaking wet, nearly falling over backwards trying to close the door behind her against the force of the wind. She approached the end of the kitchen table awkwardly with a look of confusion on her face. She refused to make eye contact with anyone at the table.

"They just threw me out of the car," Ruby said in disbelief to the floor in front of her.

She had slurred every word.

"Why would they do that?" Her gaze swung across the room but her eyes refused to focus.

"Who threw you out of the car?" Nans asked without sympathy.

"What?"

"Your friends threw you out of a car?" Nans asked.

"They are not my friends."

Ruby placed her hand on the back of her chair to steady herself and then slowly sat down in her seat, sideways. Her drenched hair dripped water down her face and formed a puddle on her plate.

"Look at me," Nans said.

"I don't want to," Ruby said almost silently.

"Look at me." Nans banged her fist on the table.

Ruby lifted her head but her eyes strayed.

"Are you on drugs?" Nans asked.

Before Ruby had a chance to answer Nans was already on her feet.

"You will not be at this table, or under my roof like this," Nans said.

"But…"

"Get out," Nans ordered.

"I can't go outside. It's not safe out there," Ruby said.

"If you don't leave right now, it won't be safe in here," Nans threatened.

"Please."

"Get out."

"No," Ruby said softly, shaking her head.

Skyler gripped her fork in her hand and scowled at her sister.

"I hate you," she hissed through clenched teeth.

Thunder rumbled ominously over the house.

"What did you say to me?"

"I hate you," Skyler said again.

"Why do you hate me?"

"You killed Parker."

"Excuse me?"

"They were your drugs that killed him. You killed our brother."

Ruby clumsily pushed herself to her feet and threw a high-arching punch at her sister. Skyler ducked in her chair and Ruby twisted herself around behind her flying fist and fell over sideways, knocking her head against the corner of the table. Skyler stood and raised a fist, ready to fight, but saw that her sister was face down and unmoving. Nans and Pops rushed passed Skyler to get to Ruby, accidentally bumping into Skyler and slamming her head back, denting the wall. As Skyler bent over clutching at her head with her hands, Pops rolled Ruby onto her back. She was unresponsive with a long cut through her right eyebrow.

"Goddamnit!" Pops cried out in frustration. Nans looked at her husband in shock, then to the window, and then crossed herself with her hand. Skyler stared down at her sister's pale face in an angry rage. With a seething scream, she exploded out of the back door and disappeared headfirst into the storm.

Boy did not wait for cowardice to come and control him. He didn't give his mind enough time to scare him. He needed to catch Skyler before she got to where she was going. Boy could sense the tragedy looming and his body carried him out of the door and directly towards it. Boy ran faster than he ever had before. His feet were barely touching the ground. Boy felt like he was flying; like he was faster than the rain and quicker than the lightning. He felt guilty for having self-centered thoughts at such a time, but his mind was racing with him. He imagined that Elle was running beside him, smiling at him, and that he was smiling back. He wanted her to be there with him. He almost felt happy to be running against the rain with her. Boy was falling in love with Elle – perhaps he had already fallen, but it was in this moment that he realized it. He had fallen in love with the idea of her, which was all that he had left of her – but it was such a beautiful idea, so clever, so unique. She was an idea he wished was his own. Each synchronized step they took he imagined them to be growing younger, growing young together, until they were just two children playing in the rain. What a time it was for love.

Boy approached the edge of the quarry with caution and kept his distance from Skyler who stood with her feet kissing the ledge. She rocked back and forth ever so slightly, staring out over the ink black water. Lightning cut jagged scars into the sky and Boy could feel the thunder rumbling beneath their feet. Boy caught his breath, inhaling the perplexing serenity of the scene. It was such a beautiful performance. He knew this is where she would be watching from.

"What do you think would happen if I jumped?" Skyler yelled out over the deafening noise of the falling rain.

"Do you think I would fly?" She looked back over her shoulder at Boy who was just another shadow in the night.

"I think I would fly," Skyler said with her chin high.

Skyler lifted her arms high at her side and closed her eyes.

Boy wondered how high she could fly.

Skyler clenched her fists and screamed until her lungs were empty. Boy listened to her roar become swallowed by the stomach of the storm. He stepped next to her and placed his hand on her shoulder. Skyler turned and unleashed another scream into his face. Boy could feel her rage becoming one with the turbulence around her. The skies were changing.

Boy realized what he was witnessing. It was neither the rain nor the wind; it was neither the thunder's rumble nor the lightning's strike; *she* was the force he felt. There was no fire, but fury that burned beneath the cowering stars. The disturbance in the air was a disturbance of the soul, a heart beating and breaking like a quake of the earth. If the trees were to bend and snap he could not blame a hurricane but only the pain that blew through her. The gravity of her agony pulled the tears from the clouds that belonged to her eyes. Everything was natural about the disaster that he stood face to face with. Boy would forever remember his epiphany, standing in front of her as she emptied her anger the night their half-built home nearly came crashing down: she was the storm, and oh, what a storm she was.

***

Boy stood in front of the fridge with his hands shoved into his pockets, studying the collage of photos that were hanging loosely from their magnets. There was so much happiness captured in the film. *Trapped rather*, Boy thought, because one could not release it when they needed it most. This thought helped to explain to Boy the paradox of sadness that comes with reminiscing on happiness that has passed away. Boy was always fascinated with old family photos, mainly because he had none of his own, but also because they served as proof that better times existed. Conversely, there was no evidence that Boy's memories were not completely imagined, created from nostalgia for times that he never had.

Boy took his time scanning the assortment of moments until he found the photo he hoped had been taken. Beneath the glossy surface there was Parker, sitting amongst the branches of a thick tree with his legs wrapped in a blanket. Parker had a buzzed head and a skinny face. His ears were pierced and his infectious smile seemed to be a perfect balance of both of his sisters'. He was wearing a black sweater with the figure of a red balloon sewed onto the front. Parker was giving a thumbs up to the camera. In the bottom corner of the frame there was a blurred hand waving excitedly at him. Boy carefully slid the photograph off of the fridge and held it delicately in his fingers.

Boy glanced over his shoulder and saw Pops and Nans holding hands, praying with their heads down at the end of the kitchen table. Boy looked up at the ceiling above them and wondered if their message was getting through. It was paradoxical how scared yet strong they looked as they said their prayers. Boy folded his own hands in front of him, holding the photo between his two palms, peeked upwards and then forced his eyes closed. His head slowly fell to his hands and the sides of his fingers pressed against his forehead. He silenced his mind and he waited.

Boy didn't want to be the first one to speak. He felt like he was being watched from the inside. He was nervous to say the wrong words or ask for too much, ashamed of not knowing how to address whoever was listening, and embarrassed to think that nobody was. Boy pulled his hands away from his face. God would not hear his silence.

What could anybody do for them? Boy wondered, looking back at Nans and Pops, hanging the photograph back onto the fridge. Perhaps there was nothing that could truly be done, but Boy was going to try and help regardless, and he was going to do it the only way that he knew how.

Boy slipped out of the kitchen and made his way down the hallway to the girls' room where Skyler and Ruby sat silently at the ends of their beds. As Boy approached the doorway, Mr. Man slid in front of him and blocked his path. His face was twisted with concern and his typically condescending voice was overtaken by worry. "I beg you to reconsider," he began.

Boy sighed at his inability to control his thoughts. He took another step forward but was halted once more by Mr. Man, who had stretched himself out in front of the doorway.

"I know what you are thinking, and I must advise you to think a different thought. You don't have much left." Mr. Man gestured at the colored marks on Boy's collar.

Boy noticed that a lock of hair had fallen loose on Mr. Man's head and he had not bothered to fix it. This gave Boy more hesitation than Mr. Man's plea, but he had already accepted that Mr. Man had been right all along. Reality was bleeding him dry and there was not much left to bleed.

"You could lose it all," Mr. Man stammered.

Boy nodded.

A boy who had nothing could not be threatened by the idea of losing everything.

Boy dismissed Mr. Man and knocked on the inside of the ajar door of the bedroom. Ruby sat staring at the ceiling, her hair pulled up out of the way of the large bandage that covered the right side of her face.

Skyler sat staring at the floor in front of her, wrapped in a towel and shivering from the chill. As Boy entered with his arms folded behind his back, the two girls brought their eyes towards him wordlessly. He detoured around their beds and stopped in front of a mirrored vanity that was lit around its edges by small lightbulbs. Boy stared at the stranger in his reflection. The boy staring back at him was emotionless; his shirt was stained and his eyes were dull. Boy let several hollowed minutes pass acknowledging who the mirror said he was, accepting what was left of himself. Then, when Boy had seen all that he needed to see, he sat himself between the girls, took each of them by the hand, and closed his eyes. Their world was waiting for them.

***

"Where are we?" Skyler's small voice rang out through the thick darkness.

The black air carried a buzz of energy, a steady hum of restless activity that could be felt but not seen. Ruby took hold of the back of Skyler's shirt and Skyler reached back and held her wrist. Connected, they took a blind step forward and then froze as they felt the dirt shifting beneath their feet. One by one, an endless stream of curvaceous, neon beetles wiggled themselves out of spiral holes in the ground and marched in unison past the sisters. They paraded in perfect order, up and over the girls' shoes while the few stragglers took a short cut between their legs. Skyler crouched down and gave them an incredulous wave. The procession of strutting beetles intersected with hundreds of other lines of hustling insects until there were millions of bug feet drumming against the soil.

All at once, the marvelous march halted in formation facing the horizon, patiently waiting for the sun to bring life to the day. As the first sliver of light scraped across the skyline, the garden came alive. Dormant, larger than life flowers sprung up and blossomed in all directions. Their petals fluttered in the gentle breeze that passed above the girls' heads. Giant bees the size of propeller planes soared in from the distance and landed acrobatically on the enchanted flowers. The cresting sun's light reflected off of the painted sky, creating a masterpiece of cracked colors like a Monet impression. Cool breezes blew across dyed ponds and puffed rainbows of pollen over the sculptured hedges.

Despite all of the garden's magical tricks, the servile beetles did not move from their positions, waiting faithfully in front of a field of sunflowers that housed a lonely tree. Skyler and Ruby stepped carefully around the beetles and sat on a pair of polka dotted mushrooms at their side. Boy stood far behind the picture, watching the anticipated arrival from over their shoulders.

The gnarled tree that rose above the flowers of the sun twisted at its trunk and turned itself around, revealing its secret slowly. Swinging his legs from a thick branch in the tree, with a blanket laid across his lap, was Parker. The tree folded over to the ground and he stepped down softly. The sisters rushed towards their brother and threw themselves in his arms. Parker flashed his toothy smile as he took turns giving them hugs and kisses between the flowers. Boy turned away to give them their privacy as Parker led his long-lost sisters through their magic garden.

Boy could feel his heart sigh knowing how serenely they strolled together. This could be their closure. The world had stolen from them and he was giving back what had been taken. He was giving them a goodbye. He was giving them the only thing he could think to give. He was giving everything he had left. He was giving it all away.

A hand swooped down from the sky and ruffled Boy's hair with a playful push. There was Elle, floating in front of him with two painted butterfly wings sticking out of her back. Boy thought it was the most beautiful combination of creatures that could ever be. She was fluttering teasingly around and over him, just out of his reach, taunting him to play with her, when out of the corner of Boy's eye he saw movement that he had not imagined. It was Mr. Man, in his white pinstripe suit, on his hands and knees in the dirt holding a dead gray flower. He was trying desperately to shove it back into the earth. He was disheveled and distraught, doing everything in his power to bring the wilted flower back to life. Leo appeared beside him, his clothes still dripping wet with the river's water. He looked frantically from the flower to Boy.

"We can fix this," he said, dropping to a knee in the dirt.

Leo pulled his wet sweatshirt away from his body and twisted the corner over the dead flower. He wrung out the water on the drooping petals and at the base of the stem in the soil. They waited for the flower to react, to jump back to life, but a dead flower would never bloom.

Mr. Man dug his fingers into the earth and lifted the flower from the loose dirt. He handed it to Boy.

"I'm sorry for your loss."

Boy accepted the flower. It felt cold in his fingers, like a corpse.

All things that live must die. Mr. Man had warned Boy in his mansion, and now it was death that grew in his garden. Before Boy could mourn, his attention was pulled violently to a fight that had broken out behind him. Parker was on his knees trying to console Skyler who was pounding on his chest and screaming. Ruby was yelling down at her sister and trying to rip them apart. Boy could hear pleading cries for answers – for a reason that Parker left them, a reason that Boy did not have.

The harder Skyler pounded the more Boy's mind shook, and as it did the vibrant colors dissolved from the garden. Boy watched on in horror as his imagination faded before him, leaving only splotches of faint colors scattered throughout. His world now resembled the bleached world that he used to escape from.

The dead flower hung its head over the edge of Boy's hand. If he was responsible for life, then he must be punished for death. If the flower had blood to bleed it would have bled on Boy's hands. There would be no funeral. Boy closed his eyes and made it all disappear.

Chapter 18: Entering the Abyss Part 1

There was no grace. There was no argument. There was no appetite. There was only a traumatized hush cast across the dinner table. Boy's fork hung limply between his idle fingers, his conscious buried beneath layers of guilt. He had upset the balance in his attempt to stabilize it. The family had always faltered but never fallen, yet everyone was deeply shaken by the storm that had passed through. This new home in this new place was meant to be their fresh start, but it did not take long for their past to find their new address. Boy took the blame, whether it belonged to him or not. Once again he had failed to be a hero, and for that he felt responsible. Boy left his plate full of food and walked away from the table. Skyler watched him from the corner of her eye as he brought his backpack out to the porch swing.

This had not been the hero's journey that he had hoped for the night he snuck out of 84 D over a month ago. The journal tucked away in his backpack still had empty pages and there were no words left to write. A childish prophecy, a deceptive destiny, had tortured him for so many years and had caused harm to many others. His catastrophic adventure was more an exploration of suffering than it was a valiant quest. From all that Boy had seen, it did not seem that there was a perfect plan for pain. Misery was monotonous and coping was confusing and futile. No one knew how to suffer.

Miss Jennie tried to hide in her past. Leo blinded himself to the fact that not all problems could be solved. Mr. Man could not confront the pain of the world so he created his own without pain and locked himself away in it. Nans and Pops forced religion yet had little faith. Skyler tried to physically fight off her feelings and Ruby drugged herself numb to avoid feeling anything at all. Boy was at a loss. He did not know what to do with the pain of the ones he loved. He accepted and subjected himself to their grief, but refused to recognize his own. His mother's final words crept back to him, a question that still demanded an answer: Who was going to save the boy with the bandana?

Boy didn't know.

However, there was one lesson that pain had taught him, and coincidentally, it was excruciating to accept. Boy had learned that very few experiences in life were more painful than realization. The loss of love or a loved one was in essence the same pain, as realization often comes in the form of death, of a dream or an idea, or rather the idea of who one dreamed to be. Understanding that he would not become who he always imagined himself to be, Boy realized that the life he lived in his mind would run parallel to the life he lived in actuality, forever. Their paths would never cross. Boy had created an idol of himself and held this idealized figure sacred, more precious than his own being, for it was created by his deepest dreams and conceptions of his own potential. He who he was and he who he wished to be had finally become enemies.

Mr. Man appeared beside Boy's thoughts. He was explicitly fatigued, with his posture slouched, and his eyes drooping lazily. He spoke in slow, staggered puzzle pieces like a drunken philosopher. "A plagiarized life can be lived and written by the same author. Creativity lacks authenticity when it is yourself you attempt to create. You have nothing left to regret."

Mr. Man fixed his tie as Boy considered his enigmatic consolations.

"They are your thoughts," Mr. Man added.

"But as always you don't want to claim them. Thus, I must speak them for you. I am sorry if they displease you."

Mr. Man crossed his legs, folded his hands in his lap and waited.

"I don't believe that it would be inaccurate for me to confess that I know how you feel. Reality is a virus to the imagination. Once you are infected, once you know exactly how things are, you struggle to imagine them how they are not. Originality becomes an impossibility. You begin to trace back every idea you have ever had to someone else's. All of those connections create a web that entraps you. Individuality becomes a delusion, because now that you see the world the same way as everyone else, you look in the mirror and see yourself the way that the world does. A dreamer cannot afford to see himself the way that others see him. Better to be blind."

Mr. Man pulled at his collar.

"Better to pack all of your dreams into a box and live in it, in a decrepit alleyway beneath a leaky air conditioner."

Mr. Man forced a smile.

"If one could control how an adventure began and ended, it would not result in an adventure at all. I admire all that you have endeavored. It must be said that there is a profound part of me that wishes you had been there in my life to try and save me, so many years ago, as I now am trying to save you."

Mr. Man stood and straightened down his suit after resting his case.

Boy looked to his side to hear what Elle had to say or what advice she could give him, to see if her energy could bring his dream back to life as it did when they first met. He waited for her, on the edge of his abyss, but she never showed.

He nodded. Absence was an answer.

Boy swung his backpack over his shoulders and followed Mr. Man towards the road without looking back.

If one was watching from the stars Boy so often gazed upon, they would believe the lone boy trudging into the darkness to be beginning another grand journey. This was exactly the opposite. Boy had finally accepted that his story would end without an ending, which was perhaps a dramatic ending in itself. The world would not miss a hero that it never had.

Chapter 19: Entering the Abyss Part 2

Boy sat on the chipped curb in front of the gas station chewing the end of his plastic yellow straw, inflating and deflating his empty juice box mindlessly. His eyes squinted against the concrete reflections of the sun and examined his surroundings. There weren't many cars, or many people, or much of anything at all for as far as Boy could see. It seemed to Boy that he had drifted to the middle of nowhere, and it also seemed to Boy that maybe this was a bad idea. Sneaking off into the night in a metaphorical surrender to the universe with no plan or resources was perhaps more of a symbolic gesture than a successful strategy. All Boy wanted was to lock himself away and stare out of his crooked window the way he did before this misadventure. But Boy was a long way away from his cage.

The redundant bell of the gas station rang and each time it did Boy flinched, because after using the restroom he had stolen the juice box he was sipping on his way out of that very door. Boy half hoped that the police would come arrest him for his petty theft and expedite his journey back to 84 D, but he was not thrilled by the prospect of potentially being thrown in a juvenile cell without windows. Boy also wished he had stolen something more substantial than a juice box if he were to be arrested, but he had rashly opted to pay an unlawful tribute to Elle and her bottomless suitcase.

The gas station bell rung again and it was followed not by the sounds of sirens, but by a striking end to what must have been a very strange conversation.

"It turns out he was actually a paranoid schizophrenic who was smuggling drugs across the border to then sell to himself. So he was a drug addict, but he was his own dealer, and Dr. Salamandro was his alias, but it was also the name of his therapist, to who he confessed that he had a drug habit but never could remember buying the drugs. The police targeted his therapist because they were searching for a suspect with his name, but when they went to arrest him he was in the middle of a session with the fake Dr. Salamandro and the police solved two crimes in one. The most ironic part is that he was given two life sentences in prison, which just goes to show that the judge had a good sense of humor."

Boy slowed the chewing of his straw momentarily and gazed interestedly at the couple making their way out of the gas station, their arms overflowing with snacks. They were a youthful pair, in both age and vitality, but the girl was exceptionally unique in appearance. She wore a golden straw hat pushed down onto waves of light brown hair. She had clusters of sunspots gathered beneath big hazel eyes, plump curved lips that rested one on top of the other, and large winged ears.

The two strangers carried their conversation towards Boy and let their collection of junk food spill onto the ground next to him.

"Why didn't you ask for a bag?" the girl asked, crossing her arms.

"Because they charge you five cents for it. We can save that money and invest it," the boy said, studying the snacks.

"Very smart," the girl replied, pointing to her temple.

Boy noticed that one of the girl's long arms was covered in stick figure tattoos all the way down to her wrist. Around her neck rested an old pair of foam-padded earphones with the cord dangling down her back. Up close, the girl had the pleasing proportions of an anime caricature. Her face was both tangibly and intangibly soft, almost to the point of conveying sadness. The boy next to her was physically her opposite. His features were dark with depth; he had mixed color skin with absorbent brown eyes. His profile was defined with hard, cutting lines like a cubist painting and his long charcoal colored curls rested on his broad shoulders.

"The real question, which you still have not answered, is whether you believe that a fully grown giraffe could beat a fully grown elephant in a fight."

"I already told you that I don't want to answer a question that involves imagining animals mauling each other."

"You don't have to imagine it, just answer it."

"You know I like animals."

"That is the beauty of speaking hypothetically; you can say anything you want because you are talking about the possibility of something, so you aren't technically talking about anything. If we were not speaking hypothetically, if we were, let's say, discussing or even promoting then it would be morally wrong, but I am just asking *hypothetically*."

"Okay, then *hypothetically*, I'm still not answering your question."

"That is not how hypothesizing works."

"I don't care how it works. All I want is for you to pick the snacks you want so we can go."

"I thought we were going to share them all?"

"Then why did we put them all on the ground?"

"Because we didn't have a bag."

The girl palmed her face and sat directly next to Boy on the curb.

"And also because I wanted to hear your answer to the question," the boy added, sitting on the other side of Boy so that he was sandwiched between their conversation.

"Hypothetical question, you mean?"

"It is the best form of question," the boy said, nodding.

"I will answer *one* question, one hypothetical question, but only if it has nothing to do with elephants and giraffes beating each other up."

"That's fair. The answer was obvious anyways. Okay, who would win between a predator bird and a killer fish?"

"Win at what?"

"A fight to the death," the boy confirmed.

"Why do all of your scenarios involve death?"

"All hypothetical fights are to the death."

The girl stood, using Boy's shoulder to help her up.

"I think we are done here," she said, giving Boy a pat on the back and collecting the snacks.

"I don't know what was so confusing about the question," the boy said, grabbing what was left of the snacks.

"I am going to fight you to the death if you don't stop talking," the girl said.

"Hypothetically," the boy said.

"*Hypothetically*," the girl agreed.

"Do we need gas?" the boy asked.

"This would be the place to get it," the girl said.

"We should be fine."

The two headed off around the corner of the gas station and Boy couldn't help but watch them walk away, still contemplating how he should feel about his invasion of personal space.

"Hey you," the girl called out, staring at Boy blankly staring at her. Boy looked away and then back at her, as if she had just caught his attention.

"You need a lift?"

Boy looked around him to make sure he was the one she was talking to. He was, and he did in fact need a lift. It seemed too good to be true, but then again the rest of his luck seemed too unfortunate to be true, yet there he was, stranded on a gas station sidewalk. Sometimes the universe just knew what Boy needed, not that it ever actually gave it to him.

Boy nodded.

Whether the universe was going to give it to him or not, he was going to take it.

"Which way you going?"

Boy glanced at the road signs and pointed east.

The girl waved him over the best she could with her arms full of munchies. Boy approached them tentatively and she gave him a wide, innocent smile. She leaned forward with her chest and dumped the snacks into Boy's arms.

"We can split my half if you carry them." She tossed her eyebrows up and down invitingly.

"We are sharing everything," the boy walking ahead of them corrected.

The girl rolled her big eyes.

"My name is Piper," she proclaimed, and stuck out her hand.

Boy tried to shake it without letting any of the snacks fall and she pulled it away with a soft laugh.

"You don't have to shake my hand. I just wanted to see if you would try, Boy."

She pointed at Boy's shirt with a finger gun. "I read your nametag."

Piper pulled the trigger.

"Pleasure to meet you, Boy. That is London."

London turned around and gave Boy a slight bow while walking backwards.

"And this is our home," Piper said.

Boy had distractedly not realized that they were standing in front of a short school bus parked sideways through a row of spaces. It was painted all black with a smiley face that was not smiling. All of the windows were pulled down and in white, cursive letters along the broad side of the bus it read '*The Abyss*'.

"We are nomads," Piper said proudly.

"Nihilistic nomads," London added.

"And that is what makes the name so existentially clever," Piper said.

The front door of the bus swung open with a hiss of air and London ushered them aboard. London and Piper jumped in the driver's seat, which had been modified to fit two people, and Boy sat himself in the squishy cushioned seat behind them.

"I would give you a tour but we have to hit the road because we don't have time to waste. That's a joke, all time in this life is wasted," London yelled into the rearview mirror as he started up the rumbling engine.

"There are no seatbelts on the bus, for obvious philosophical reasons, but sitting on my hands always makes me feel safer."

London gave the horn a few squeaky honks, pulled out of the parking lot and swerved widely onto the main road.

Boy was dumbfounded by how quickly everything was happening. He was also puzzled by what exactly *was* happening. Two self-proclaimed nihilistic nomads had shared an unsolicited conversation with him and then offered to bring him back across the country without Boy so much as uttering a single word. It was random, but it was the best he could expect without a plan, and certainly better than any alternative he could think of.

Boy glanced around at the inventive renovations that had been made to *The Abyss.* There remained only one row of seating on the entire bus, the rest of the space had been creatively converted into vagabond living areas. In the back of the bus there was a raised wooden platform with a large mattress and blankets thrown across it. Below the loft there was a short kitchen counter with a gas stove and a mini-fridge tucked in the corner. Directly behind Boy there was a table nailed into the side of the bus with a small television strapped down on top of it. Beneath the T.V. there was an old gaming system plugged into a bundle of electrical cords and outlets. Overhead there were several flimsy cabinets that lacked architectural integrity but somehow managed to store the majority of their belongings. A loose skateboard rolled freely down the aisle and beneath the seats. Boy caught it with his foot.

"Hey Boy, great name by the way," London called back, his eyes searching for Boy's in the mirror.

"Just wanted to give you a little introduction to our lifestyle. To keep it simple, we basically drive around in this van, all day every day, passionately without a purpose. We have come to realize that nothing really matters. We don't necessarily agree with the label of nihilism, mainly because we distrust labels, but it does summarize our essence pretty succinctly."

Piper turned around the corner of her seat with wide, excited eyes.

"You would think that not a lot of people would like us, because we come off as pretty negative when we say that everyone and everything is meaningless, but I think you would be pleasantly surprised to know that we actually make a lot of new friends on the road because the majority of people that we come across hate their lives."

"It's also a really great conversation starter. It's kind of like being vegan except people actually want to hear about it," London said.

"We aren't really anti-anything in particular, more like anti-everything. We like to paint with a broad brush," Piper said.

"But we hate idioms."

"Hate them."

"But using any strong emotional language like that gives the impression that we care enough about anything to hate something."

"Which isn't the case."

"Relentless indifference is our standard approach to opinions."

"However, there are certain types of people who irk us," Piper said.

"People who lick their fingers before rifling through papers."

"People who wear zip-off pants."

"People who triple-check things."

"People that sneeze more than twice in a row."

"People that slap their knee when they laugh."

"People who say, 'I think I blinked' after taking a picture."

"People who snap their fingers for any reason."

"People who don't acknowledge that the plural of moose should be meese."

"I am surprised there isn't more outrage around that," London said.

"We love fashion though; it gives us a fun form of expressing ourselves."

"Expressing how much we don't care about anything else."

"Precisely."

Boy felt the bus swerve quickly and a long horn blasted from the car behind them. Piper and London gave a few synchronized claps.

"One thing we like to do to entertain ourselves during long drives is give rounds of applause to anybody who honks at us or gives us the finger," London said.

"We want them to feel good about themselves for being so brave to blow their horn at us," Piper explained.

"I would say it was a coincidence that we found you, if we believed in coincidences and didn't accept the fact that some things happen in life and some things don't for no reason at all, because this is one of the rare times we are heading east with no stops," London said.

"My friend found us some work on the coast for a few months and we want to get there for the last week of summer," Piper explained.

"We work for short periods of time, save up as much money as we can and then leave before we get attached to anything. If we didn't have to work we wouldn't. I would much rather admit I am doing nothing by physically doing nothing, than slaving away at a job half the hours of the day and pretend I am making a difference," London said.

"We call jobs, 'Museums of Modern Suffering', and occasionally we take tours," Piper said.

"You might notice that our topics of conversation may seem a bit sporadic, but that is by design," London said.

"When you stop caring about life's grander questions your mind has a lot of time to ponder the more minute intricacies of our existence," Piper explained.

"The one thing I want to make very clear," London said, locking onto Boy's eyes in the mirror, "is that we are not here to become a part of your life. We don't care about who you are and we don't want you to care about us. Nothing that we say or do is a memory worth saving. There is nothing, nor anyone, inside or outside of this van, of any importance. Nothing that has happened to you or will happen to you is significant in any way. We are just a vehicle that is taking you where you tell yourself you need to go."

Piper nodded her head in subtle agreement. Boy was startled by the directness.

"When we get you to where you are going we will continue on to where we are going and that will be the end of it. We will not wish you the best in life because superlatives are inconsequential," London finished.

"But we will wish you good dental hygiene," Piper looked back over her shoulder at Boy.

"Dental hygiene is important," she smiled, showing off her white teeth.

London punched on the radio and Piper put her headphones over her ears and pressed play on her CD player. Together, yet separated, they cruised meaninglessly down the infinite road in front of them.

Boy was conflicted. He wanted to believe that the universe was giving him one last chance to save the day, to sacrifice himself, to spill his final colors for the sake of another, but this was his resignation from life living. His conscious reminded him that this was his cowardly retreat. As the nihilists had made clear, they were not going to be a part of his story. His story was already written, with extra pages left to tear out. London and Piper were nothing more than an occurrence. They just happened to cross paths with him, which wasn't a surprise to them because they understood a human's path to be a nonsensical scribble that was bound to collide with another from time to time. There was nothing special about this. Boy had to force himself to swallow the idea because it felt like one last chance, but it wasn't. So, as they barreled down the endless highway, Boy and his faded eyes allowed the picturesque landscapes to blur outside of his open window.

It didn't mean anything.

Chapter 20: Wander with Elephants

The three travelers sat squished into a rounded leather booth in the corner of a tin-can diner that they had spotted on the side of the road. Boy sat with his elbows on the table, pulling apart a deformed chicken finger over a plate of unnaturally yellow French fries. Piper people-watched the locals at the counter while she sipped her milkshake and London chewed the ice from the bottom of his empty cup.

"You know that that is bad for your teeth, right?" Piper said.

"So is smoking and eating fruit," London said.

"You don't smoke or eat fruit."

"I smoke sometimes."

"I just think you should be more conscious of your oral health."

"Food is not the enemy."

"Gingivitis can kill you."

"No it can't."

"Severe cases absolutely can."

"I have a question."

"I am sure you have more than one."

"If you could only eat one food for the rest of your life what would it be?"

Piper dipped her straw like a spoon into her glass and scooped out a chunk of un-blended ice cream.

"That question is so loosely related to the topic I feel that I shouldn't even acknowledge it."

"It's correlated."

"I would never eat only one food for the rest of my life. That sounds horrible."

"Yeah, okay, that's beside the point. The game is that you can *only* eat one food for every meal for the rest of your life."

"That sounds like a shitty game. I would never play that with you." Piper reached over and stole a soggy fry from Boy's plate.

"For goodness sake Piper, *hypothetically*…"

"I was waiting for that."

"If someone forced you to eat one thing forever what would you pick?"

"It seems strange to me that whoever is forcing me to eat the same thing every day is letting me choose my meal. I feel like they would be more controlling than that."

"You are ruining this," London said.

He pointed across to Boy for an answer. Boy, who was only half listening, held up a floppy chicken finger as a response.

"Now that is a normal answer," London said, dragging his eyes away from Boy, who looked ill.

Boy's mind no longer wandered and words seemed more worthless than ever before. The nomads spoke just to hear the sounds and Boy was struggling to embrace their philosophies. He had believed in the concept of heroism, only to be told that in life there were no heroes or villains. There were just generic beings wandering about, with wandering thoughts that lacked direction, which led to conversations that meant nothing. However, Boy wanted to be like London and Piper because they were invincible. Passion, love, aspirations – those were weaknesses, and to live a life without them was to live without vulnerability. They were protected by their impassivity and their neglect of basic human sentiments. They were safe; they had no dreams they needed to protect themselves from.

"You would get fat," Piper said, taking another long sip of her milkshake until she sucked up air.

"People get fat from eating different things every day too," London said.

"All I am saying is that you should floss more," Piper said.

"I'll say it again. Food is not the enemy."

"Bacteria is."

"Your point has been made."

London crunched on a piece of ice and flicked some cash on top of the bill.

"We are less than a week away my friends, until our little trip is over," London announced.

Boy pushed away his half-eaten meal on top of its slippery plastic placemat.

"You look so sad," London said to Boy. "You really are getting the hang of this."

Boy tossed a dirty, crumpled napkin onto his plate.

"But seriously," London said, "we all need to wash our hands before we leave."

***

The Abyss was perilously perched on the side of the road as the travelers broke to allow the traffic ahead of them to clear. They passed the time playing cards on the roof of the bus and surveying the congestion of cars fighting for inches on the highway. Neither the commuters nor the cards seemed to flow, as a dispute over gameplay forced the cards back into the deck.

"You can't change the rules when you are losing and then change them back when you are winning," Piper argued, vigilantly watching London's hands as he shuffled.

"I told you this is a flexible game," London said, flicking the back of the top card before dealing out to the reluctant players.

"It isn't a flexible game if there are no rules at all. If you had no bones you wouldn't be flexible, you would be a useless sack of stretchy skin. This game is the equivalent of that." Piper snatched the dealt cards off of the roof and held them close to her chest. She peeked over at Boy's hand and he willingly showed her his cards.

"Who is cheating now?" London asked, re-arranging the cards in his hand.

"How can we cheat if we don't even know how to play?" Piper swapped one of her twos for Boy's ace. London tossed down a card in the middle to start the game.

"Thinking about not having bones brings me back to a question that has haunted me for years," London said.

"A hypothetical question?" Piper asked.

"Of course, but it is a good one I promise. If you were to eat yourself completely, do you think that you would double in size or disappear completely?"

"Why, just why?" Piper asked, burying her face in her cards.

"It is a question that has been bothering me lately," London clarified, flicking down another card on top of the pile.

"Well it is a question that is bothering me now. It is a bothersome question."

"I know you would die before you could finish, but there are so many other problems that I just don't know how you would avoid."

"Yes, I imagine an attempt at eating yourself whole would be problematic."

Boy leaned over and picked up a card from the side pile.

"For instance, how would you eat your arm if people can't even lick their elbows? And how could you eat your mouth, with your mouth?"

"I think there are far bigger flaws with this concept than the anatomy of it, London."

"I know the question is double in size or disappear, but part of me feels like you would just weigh the same. If you ate your weight and then lost all your weight, it would balance out. Or maybe you would be losing all of your weight and then gaining it back because it takes time to digest."

"And I feel like you have thought about this more than you should have. Stop waving your cards around, I don't want to see them. I don't want you to have any excuses if you lose." Piper studied her own hand intently.

"Or would you just turn inside out?"

"You should just ask someone who has done it, they can tell you."

"If the answer is disappear then there would be no way to find them," London pointed out.

"If the answer is double in size they would be easy to spot in a crowd," Piper said.

"If the answer is turn inside out I don't think I want to meet that person."

"Maybe you should just try it and let us know how it goes."

"I win." London tossed his final card on top of Piper's.

"I quit," Piper said, discarding the rest of her hand all at once. "I am going to find a tree to pee behind."

Piper scaled down from the bus and left London and Boy alone on the roof. London looked awkwardly from Boy to the traffic. He seemed uncomfortable with Boy's direct silence and bored by the idea of waiting patiently and uneventfully.

"You like to gamble, Boy?"

London re-shuffled the cards as Boy stared at him blankly.

"Gambling is easy – all you do is bet on what you think will happen and if it happens, you win. If it doesn't happen, you lose. The only hard part is losing, but if you don't care what happens then there is nothing easier than gambling."

London placed a card down in front of Boy and a card in front of himself.

"I cannot be manipulated because I don't care what happens to me. I cannot win and I cannot lose."

Boy absorbed London's revolutionary words like a dry sponge.

"Let's play. High or low?"

Boy pointed to the blue sky above him.

"I almost forgot to ask," London held up his hand, "what are we betting? We have to feel like we are losing something to realize we have lost nothing."

London emptied his phone and his wallet from his pocket.

"If your card is higher, I throw everything off of the bus. I'll throw the deck of cards too so we can never play again."

Boy patted his empty pockets to show he had nothing of his own to risk, but London shook his head fervently.

"Not to worry," he said, swinging himself down through the bus window and scaling back up to the roof with Boy's backpack in hand. He slid Boy his bag.

"We all have something to gamble."

Boy pulled his journal out of his bag and tossed it down next to the deck of cards without hesitation. Nothing mattered anymore.

London's eyes lit up and he grabbed the edge of his card.

"It all comes and it all goes."

London flipped over a king of spades and Boy turned a seven of diamonds. Boy's empty eyes glanced from one card to the other without the slightest hint of surprise or deception. In one swooping motion, Boy lifted his leather journal into his hand and threw it off of the bus. The cover came undone midflight and the pages flapped wildly like the wings of a hunted bird. The journal crashed in a thorn-filled bush and the barbs stabbed through the words within.

London kicked the deck of cards off the bus and quickly became uninterested in his anarchic lesson. He turned his attention to the traffic clearing ahead and blew a short breath through his nose.

"Let's get going. We will be there in a few days."

***

Boy squinted at the small flashing monkey that jumped across the bulbous screen as his hands fumbled with the controller. He knew what he was supposed to be doing, but his fingers weren't cooperating and he couldn't prevent his clumsy character from getting sucker punched off of the floating stage. Boy scooched himself closer to the television and wiped his sweaty hands on his pants. Somehow he had managed to get his player stuck in a corner facing the wall, and when he pulled the joystick to go in reverse he walked off of the edge and lost his final life. His controller vibrated and the game was over.

"You suck, huh?" Piper sat with her feet up holding her controller above her head in victory.

"Don't take it personally though, he can't beat me either." She motioned at London who was half asleep in the aisle of the bus.

"Check this out," Piper said, pointing to one of her skinny tattoos on her wrist. It was a black outline of the video game character that she had just been playing with.

"It's in my blood," Piper said with a curled lip.

Boy scanned up and down her arm at all of the small symbols and images. It reminded him of cave paintings or hieroglyphics.

"You can touch them if you want, just don't wipe them off."

Boy ran a finger over the ink to see what they felt like. They felt permanent.

"I love my tattoos," Piper said fondly.

"I designed them all, which you could probably tell because I can't draw, so they are all stick figures. They aren't very artistic, but they have a lot of personality, like me. I used to get a tattoo for every big moment in my life, the ones I didn't want to forget, but then…" Piper glanced down at London lying face down, "*we* realized that there was no such thing as a big moment. Life is inconsequential and forgettable…" her voice trailed off.

Piper slapped her legs and instantly reanimated.

"I have a surprise for you."

She stood and stepped over London to grab something from her bag. She sat back down with her old CD player and her over the ear headphones.

"Books on tape."

Piper held the player up for Boy to admire.

"They are *motivational*," she whispered.

"I know it's ironic that a nihilist enjoys motivational tapes but that is why I listen to them. It makes me feel scandalous." Piper flashed a quick smile but it disappeared just as quickly.

"They are my guilty pleasure," she added, placing the headphones over Boy's ears.

"This is the best one. It's called 'Wander with Elephants'; it's a book of inspirational poems. Do you like poems?"

Boy nodded. He had become a big fan of poetry.

"I want you to hear this."

Piper pushed in the play button and a soft static sounded in his ears. Boy let his fingers fall open and imagined Elle's hand holding his own. He stared at his feet as a gentle voice began to speak:

"To stay relevant,
Or wander with elephants,
Difficult to decide harder to describe with elegance,
Hiding from the lights of the night that guide us,
Fighting my shadow to keep quiet
So that they may never find us,
Sleeves short so the scars from our battles remind us,
To breathe deep and smile with ease,
Never forget the thank you's after the please,
I hope not to lose it,
Hope that is,
Love the words that are spoken
But hate the man that spoke it,
Laughter all around me
But I can never find where the joke is,
Obsessed with possessions,

Possessed by obsessions,
Expelled by the teachers and reverends
So I could carry the message
I am learning the lessons,
I wish this train put me to sleep,
Living with less than a lease,
Found my home in the streets,
Finally ended the war with my peace,
So, the only question is,
Do I stay relevant?
Or go and wander with elephants?"

The headphones buzzed with a heavy emptiness as the tape ended. Piper had rested her head on Boy's shoulder and closed her eyes. She reached up and pulled the headphones down around his neck.

"I listen to that poem every night. I understand the question he is asking, but I hate that he doesn't answer it."

Piper lifted her head from Boy's shoulder and rubbed her finger along the ink on her arm.

"I didn't want to disappear from my life, but I vanished."

Piper picked up the video game controller, tossing it back and forth between her hands.

"Where did I go? How do I find me?"

She leaned forward and placed her elbows on her knees.

"I loved my life, Boy. I don't know why I left it. They say you never know what you have until it's gone, but I always knew that what I had was special, but maybe that makes it worse. Knowing how great something is makes you constantly afraid to lose it."

Piper turned her sad, cartoon eyes up at Boy.

"It's like torture. A beautiful torture."

Piper laid the controller on the floor in front of her. She looked down at London, sleeping in the bus aisle.

"I used to believe everything he told me. I don't believe him anymore."

Piper stared back at the glowing television full of characters waiting to fight.

"I think you needed to meet us. We might just be taking you back to where you started, but it might be just where you need to go."

Boy turned his face to the glowing screen.

"Maybe we are the answer to a question you have. Or maybe we are the wrong answer, but that could be just as useful. Process of elimination."

Piper stole a glance at Boy who stole a glance back at her.

"You want to know the truth, Boy? I care about everything. I thought it would be easier, once life got hard, to not care about anything. He convinced me of that. He was trying to protect me. But this pretending is worse than the pain ever was. This is all so pointless. At least the pain had a purpose."

Piper reached forward and shut off the television.

"I am leaving him. I need to be on my own for a while. At the end of the day, I am all I really have.

London rolled over with a yawn and rubbed his eyes. Piper put a finger in front of her lips.

"One last thing," she said, reaching beneath the lone seat of the bus.

"Be careful where you leave your things," she handed Boy his scuffed journal. "I almost peed on it."

Boy's mind had been deceitful, but his heart knew what he needed. He took his journal from her and tucked it under his arm.

"Ink is permanent, Boy."

Piper dropped her hand from her mouth, and loaded her finger gun with a smile. She shot it into the air with finality.

"Get some sleep, Boy. I can't remember where we are going, but we will be there tomorrow."

Chapter 21: Skeleton Desert

The nausea expanding throughout Boy's stomach confirmed that everyone was anxious to finish off the road trip, as they were only a few hours away from the address he had written down. The bus swung and rocked like a ship in a storm and Boy was becoming seasick. Their reckless driving elicited a symphony of abusive honks and hand gestures from the cars that they narrowly passed, and true to form the travelers applauded them all in return. It sounded like a standing ovation.

London in particular seemed motivated to conclude the long journey, or at least Boy assessed by his lack of braking. London's overflowing energy spewed into his anti-imperial rant that had dominated the conversation of the morning.

"The whole concept is artificial. Being a 'good driver' has nothing to do with actual motor skill – and I am referring to the brain not the engine – but has instead been perverted to an evaluation of your submissiveness. You are forced to pathetically surrender to tyrannical laws based on the government's hunger for controlling our freedom of movement. When I refuse to submit to the will of the oppressor, I am classified as a bad driver, not based on my actual capabilities but on whether or not I adhered to the traffic signals. If anyone ever complains about my driving in this bus I will make them walk. I get people from where they were to where they are going. Is that not the reason they got on the bus? If they are scared, they should have had me drop them off at a church," London spewed.

"Personally, I don't think it is oppressive to use a turn signal," Piper said, pulling her headphones down around her neck.

She took a long swig of her iced tea and then rolled the bottle down the aisle to Boy who picked it up and took a sip.

"You can still go wherever you want. The turn signals just tell what direction you are going. I don't think there is anything inherently authoritarian in that," Piper said.

"Perhaps not. However, I will never yield to the traffic," London said.

"Of course not, nobody does. How do you feel about the carpool lane?" Piper asked.

"Don't even get me started about the carpool lane."

The bus grumbled as London pressed the accelerator and reached over to turn up the radio. Suddenly, there was a moment of panic in which the bus swerved recklessly into the adjacent lane and then veered off onto the shoulder of the road. Piper helped London regain control but not before a distinct 'thud' came from under the front tire. London slammed a fist onto the dashboard and switched on the hazard lights.

"We hit something," he said, pulling over to the side of the road. The co-drivers stepped down from the bus to assess the damage and Boy tried to take advantage of the stop to settle his stomach, but the sinking reality of returning to 84 D was equally as nauseating. Miss Jennie's punishments would be heartless, relentless, and mercilessly ingenious. Boy imagined her seething and brooding, fantasizing about tortures that would make even the most sadistic shudder.

He had yet to find a solution to suffering and his traumas remained unaddressed. He had taste-tested coping mechanisms as if he had been choosing a flavor of ice cream, and piled the pain of others on top of his own until it was buried alive. Now he found himself on his way back to where he started as the antagonist of his own story. Boy's thoughts were not helping ease his stomach.

Boy exited the bus and joined London and Piper by the side of the road. They were huddled together about one hundred feet behind the bus, staring down at the ground. Boy shoved his hands in his pockets and stepped between them to see what they were hovering over. Lying mangled and alone on the hot asphalt was a butchered rabbit. Its mouth hung slightly open, its legs were contorted, and its brown fur was splattered with red.

"It's dead," London said.

"It's dead," Piper confirmed.

The two nomads turned with a nod and walked away but Boy stayed behind with the slain rabbit. The cowardly voice inside of his head tried to convince him that this did not matter. The painless philosophy would teach that the loss of this innocent creature, once alive and now dead, was not a tragedy. Boy did not believe that. A life had come to a sudden and unjust end and no one would grieve. No one would even know what had been lost. The body would rot and the bones would be left unburied on the asphalt. Boy had to be the one to mourn, but he did not know how much more his heart could hold, or how many more bones he could carry.

Boy bent down and slid his hands under the rabbit's body. He lifted it carefully and held it gently beneath its limp neck. Its fur was not as soft as he imagined it would be. As Boy cradled the rabbit in his arms, his faded eyes began to turn slowly like rusted gears. The world went silent. It was as if he could hear the absence of the rabbit's heartbeat. Then, grain by grain, a storm of sand began to kick up around him. It swirled and flurried, scratching away at the sky. A desert was forming in the barren wasteland of his imagination. There was no color. There was black sand with blinding white light in the sky. The rabbit's body had become a skeleton in his arms. Boy scanned across the lonely dunes and saw that his mind had filled with unburied bones. There were no faces or flesh, only the bare frames of beings and ideas that ceased to be, staggering through the shifting sands, all pushing straight ahead. It was a fantastic exodus.

Boy lifted his chin and took his first step forward.

"Give me death."

Elle Lavender was at his side with her finger in the air. Her velvet dress was bleached colorless.

"I want to die a slow death,
If life has a beginning and an end, then so my friend must death,
As we begin to live we begin to die,
Thus when life is finished then so is death,
So let me die slowly,
Please let me make it last,
Let me die slowly,
Because life is far too fast."

As Elle recited her poem, Boy could see the remnants of his fantasies sticking out of the sand – discarded, forgotten, and abandoned. He walked past shards of glass from the jar which held his fireflies. He saw strands of melted clouds from his final dance, the handle of a sword from his knightly quests, and dead flowers that had wilted in his magic garden. He stepped sorrowfully around Leo's rocket, crashed far from its home in space.

"Life and death, I believe they are the same,
But if I had to choose between the two I swear and swear again,
I would scream: Give me death! Give me death! Give me death!
For to learn what it means to have life,
I believe that I need to lose it,
I for too long have tried to hold it to me closely,
If I had one last wish
It would be
That you take it from me slowly."

As they trudged through the skeleton desert Boy could feel the pulsing sun burning his hands that held the bones. He was afraid that he would drop them in the sand. Elle paused her poem and pointed to the path that Boy had created behind him. Marching in procession, following his footsteps in the sand, was everyone he had ever shared his world with. They stood in single file with their eyes cast down, carrying their own skeletons without a word. Boy continued forward.

"I apologize,
For all of my final words,
Now I empathize,
With the silent mockingbird,
To all my loved ones, I hope you read this letter,
Please pray to your god that I die a slow, infinite death,
So that I may live forever."

Elle's voice was taken by the wind and the characters of Boy's story stopped in their tracks. They had reached the end of their mirage. All that remained of the infinite desert was a rope bridge that swung above a bottomless chasm. It was a bridge with no visible end and no promise from the other side. Boy's weary eyes examined all of the faces that had lived with him within his mind. It was the curtain call of his imagination. There was Ruby and Skyler, Leo, Mr. Man, Elle, and his mother wearing her bandana. There they stood – the prisoners of his mind that had held him captive. It was time for them to make their way off his stage.

"Let them bury their bones," Elle said.

Boy gave a humble, thankful nod to Elle and then another to those standing in the sand. Boy stepped to the side and cleared an entrance to the bridge. One by one they made their way to the edge of Boy's consciousness. Skyler and Ruby crossed first. Boy gave them a subtle wave as they passed him. Leo, dripping wet despite the desert heat, pointed to the sky above him as he made his exit. Mr. Man approached the bridge and paused to groom himself to perfection. He gave Boy a nod and said, "The only man who never died is the man who never lived. It was an honor to do both," and then proudly crossed the bridge.

Elle stood shoulder to shoulder with Boy's mother. She gave her a kiss on the cheek, transferring his mother's bones into her arms, and then took the skeleton out of Boy's hands.

"I can carry yours for now."

Elle gave Boy a wink, turned to the bridge, and carried the bones across.

Boy stood alone with his mother; a mother that he had not imagined in a very long time. He had been afraid that he would mistake her details and picture a mother that wasn't his own. He was embarrassed as well – nervous that she may not recognize his imagination after all of the color it had lost. Yet there she was, beautiful in black and white. There was her smile like the summer wave, crashing on the shores of his desert.

Boy looked from his mother to his graveyard of fantasies with a mixture of resentment and remorse. There laid all that was and could have been. At his feet he saw his unfinished journal plunged into the sand. Boy picked it up and brushed off the cover but couldn't bring himself to open it.

"You couldn't have saved me, baby."

Boy's mother took the journal from his trembling hands and dropped it back to the sand.

"It's not your fault. I was supposed to save you."

Boy shoved his hands into his pocket as tears welled in his eyes.

"You were only a boy."

Boy dug his face into her neck and collapsed into her arms. He wanted to be her hero the way that she was his.

"Who is going to save the boy with the bandana?"

His mother planted a long kiss on the top of his head.

"You are."

Boy broke down and began to cry, slipping from his mother's arms and falling to his knees in the sand. He cried and cried until he had no more colors left to lose and had only water left for tears.

Boy wept.

As he flushed out his soul the sky began to change. He cried himself empty until the clouds were full above him. Boy's mother proudly watched her son embrace his pain as she tightened her bandana around her head.

"Hey, you aren't writing any of this down."

His mom stepped onto the swinging bridge and left her son to become the hero he needed to be.

"Let your heart suffer," she said as she disappeared behind the flurrying wall of sand.

As the tears ran down his face, drop by drop, the colors rained back down into his mind. The mockingbird swooped down from the painted sky singing his song and from the depths of the desert life began to grow anew.

Chapter 22: Saving Grace

Boy was going to wait until he had the perfect words to write before he put the pen to paper, but he knew that he had nothing perfect to say. What he had to write was raw and flawed. However, it was the truth, and not one he had imagined for himself. There was no perfect ending to his story, nor had there been an optimal beginning, but the pages would be filled. His story would be written. Boy did not actually believe in perfect endings because nothing perfect would ever end, but his story was imperfect in every way, and thus, it must conclude.

Boy tapped his pen on the final page with a newfound patience. He sat on the concrete steps where *The Abyss* had spit him out. As promised, the nomads had delivered him to where he believed he needed to be and then disappeared back into their meaningless existence. Boy buried his mind between the blank lines and searched for the words to explain his epiphany. For far too many years, Boy had imagined himself to be a boy with a bandana looking for someone to save, when all along it was he who needed a hero. Boy clicked the back of his pen and wrote down his final words. He read them over doubtfully. They seemed to be too simple. There was too much complexion in his story to settle for a simple summary. Or perhaps, in essence, the ending to any story was simple because it was over. There was nothing left to say and that is why it had to end.

Before Boy closed the leather cover he flipped back through the pages to where it all began. His story was a potent blend of fantasy and reality, told true to how he had lived it. Words that were written with pain were now read with appreciation. Boy was thankful for the universe's creativity. He could have never imagined all that had happened to him. It had given him an invaluable story and now it was time to share that story. That was the real reason Boy was sitting on the porch of 84 D. He wanted to give his journal to the person who he needed to hear his voice, a stranger he felt deeply connected to, a person he grew up with, a rare constant in his life – the other face he had seen in the flames. It was someone who was a part of his story even though her name wasn't written in the pages. The truth was that he didn't even know her name, but the girl who lived on the other side of the window would soon know his.

Boy walked across the street confidently although he was not sure how to communicate what the journal was or why it was for her. To Boy it was his prized possession, but to the watching world it was nothing more than a worn down notebook filled with fantasized tales written with poor penmanship. Boy's feet carried him faster than his thoughts could process and before he knew it he was standing in front of his old neighbor's door. Boy debated his options and decided to leave the journal on the doorstep and ring the bell. He laid the journal down gently on the mat but then thought it rude to leave such a confusing gift without context. Also, he wanted her to know that he wrote it. Boy picked the journal back up. Then he imagined trying to navigate the impending conversation and ultimately elected to lay the journal back on the stoop.

Boy floated his finger over the doorbell, but before he had the chance to ring it the door was thrown open and the strawberry blonde haired girl stumbled clumsily out of the house. She was trying to drag a half-zipped suitcase out of the door, but was tripping over the loose clothes that were spilling onto the ground. Boy instinctively reached down to help the girl but his presence surprised her, causing her to drop even more of her belongings. The girl's cheeks reddened as she corralled her clothes and forced her suitcase to close with an exasperated grunt. She stared at Boy distrustfully and waited for him to speak. If she hadn't had recognized him, she may have waited forever.

"You used to live across the street," the girl said. "In the foster home."

The girl's voice was airy and approachable, as Boy imagined it would be.

"I used to see you in the window. I recognize your eyes." She squinted to get a closer look at Boy's freshly painted irises.

"They are even brighter up close," she commented with a disarming smile.

"I'm sad we aren't neighbors anymore. I heard they shut down the foster home a few days ago."

Boy raised his eyebrows. He had been so immersed in the ending of his story that he had not realized that 84 D had come to its own conclusion. The house was abandoned and the crooked window from which he used to watch the world was boarded up. Boy didn't think that happiness nor sadness was the right emotion to feel, but he felt something in between the two.

"My parents said they were forced to close it. Fire code violations."

Boy laughed dryly. Leo would have loved to see it.

"The lady who lived there sold the house to the city and moved. I don't know where she went, but I think they are going to tear it down. They want to buy ours too, in order to urbanize the whole city, but my parents won't sell. We are our own neighborhood now."

Boy thought of Miss Jennie and her faded clothes. He wouldn't go as far as saying he missed her, but being away helped him understand her as a human. She wasn't the only one who didn't know how to handle the life she was given or the life that was taken from her.

Boy looked back to the girl from the other side of the window and shrugged. The girl shrugged back and laid a hand delicately on her stomach. A faint sound of crying escaped from the open door behind her and Boy looked curiously over her shoulder into the home. The girl's mother had her head on the dinner table and was weeping into her hands. The father sat beside her, slouched in his chair, arms tucked across his chest. As the mother cried the father bobbed his head slowly, as if nodding in agreement. Boy's attention pulled back to the daughter's caressing hand on her stomach. Without looking back, the girl reached behind her and closed the door, dropping her other hand to the handle of her suitcase.

"You caught me at a confusing time," the girl said apologetically.

"They are really great parents, I promise. They aren't embarrassed by me, I am embarrassed by me. They have given me everything and I just can't take anything else from them. I'm kicking myself out, I don't want you to think…" the girl's voice trailed off as her eyes strayed from her stomach back to Boy.

"I am sorry for telling you all of this. You didn't ask. Is there something I can help you with? I really should be going now."

Boy, who had just finished putting together the puzzle pieces, felt like he was familiar with the story that was playing out in front of him. He picked up the journal off of the porch and handed it to her. She received it with both hands.

"What is this? Is this for me?"

Boy nodded.

"Is it a book?"

Boy nodded again.

"Why are you giving this to me?"

The girl's question went unanswered.

"Well, thank you."

The girl rubbed her thumb across the worn cover, undid the golden buttons and then flipped the journal open to one of the first pages. Her eyes scanned the words and she smiled.

"*He was the king of many castles, the slayer of dragons,*" she read aloud theatrically.

"I love fantasy," she said without looking up from the page.

Boy smiled.

"You wrote this," the girl said as she skimmed through the story and then flipped back to the start.

"There's no title," she said, finally looking up at Boy who was proudly watching her read his words.

"What's it called?" she asked.

"*The Bandana boy*," he answered.

"Does *The Bandana boy* have a happy ending? I could really use one of those right now."

Boy paused to consider if the beginning and the middle of his story were worth the finish.

He nodded. It was a perfect ending.

The girl breathed a sigh of relief and opened the journal to its final page marked with fresh ink. She ran her finger beneath the words as she read, "The boy became a hero the day he saved himself."

The girl closed the journal, buttoned it and tucked it under her arm. Her lips were pursed and her eyes were watery. Boy shoved his hands in his pockets and looked down at his burnt shoes.

"My name is Hailey Grace," she said.

"He doesn't have a name yet, so you can call him whatever you want," Hailey Grace said, tapping her stomach playfully.

"Jonathan," Boy said.

"That could be a great name for him."

"My name is Jonathan."

Hailey Grace smiled.

"What a wonderful name. I may have to borrow it."

She reached out and hugged Boy.

"Thank you. I needed this."

Hailey Grace squeezed Boy's journal into her chest.

"I will read every word," she promised.

Boy looked from the thankful eyes of Hailey Grace to the boarded up window of 84 D. He laughed at how far he had to go and how far he had to come, just to cross the street.

It was poetic justice. Or maybe it was just poetic. He wasn't sure, but he knew who he could ask.

Boy left Hailey Grace on her front steps with a humble nod. She waved him goodbye with his story in her hands. It was time for him to go and return the bandana he had borrowed when he was only a boy, but before he would do that he had to stop at a white house with a red door and see the skinniest tree anyone had ever seen. Elle's directions had been clear on how to find her, and he planned on doing so. Boy would cross the city and Elle would be waiting for him on the other side. He would have no way of knowing if the tree in her front yard was actually the skinniest in the world, but he would take her word for it.

Boy stopped in the middle of the street and turned around to face his past one last time. He looked from the hollowed 84 D back to the girl who lived on the other side of the window, but she was gone. Hailey Grace had left her suitcase on the porch and gone back inside to be with her family. It took Boy a moment to understand the weight of what had happened. A smile snuck onto his face. Just like that Hailey Grace had become a hero. She made it look so easy.

Boy let his legs carry him straight as his mind wandered. He pulled out the pen from his back pocket that had been wrapped up in the bandana. He clicked the pen open and closed, exposing the eager ink to the fading summer sun. This may have been an end but it felt much like a beginning. Boy couldn't help but wonder what his next story would entail. He began crafting the words that he would write on the first blank page of his newest narrative. He envisioned worlds inside of worlds, reality painted with imagination; he could see it all so clearly. It was all so colorful.

When the words finally arranged themselves in the perfect order in Boy's mind, he tucked the pen back into his pocket. He did not need to write them down because he knew he would never forget them:

There are millions of stories to tell and a million ways to tell each one, but the greatest story you will ever know is your own.

The End

Author Bio

Ryan Anthony Dube is a twenty-four year old creative storyteller from Manchester, CT. Ryan recognizes the influence that living a great story has on telling a great story and is in constant search of unique experiences that he can convert into creative inspiration. Ryan is an avid traveler, having traveled to over fifty countries and hundreds of cities. Ryan is passionate about learning and growth as a human being, challenging himself along the entire spectrum of creativity by dabbling in photography, videography, spoken-word poetry, dancing, music, language learning, and travel blogging. Ryan plans to chase his dreams for his entire life and hopes to never lose his perspective on the beauty of the struggle. Follow Ryan Anthony Dube on his adventures at penandpaperstories.com and on social media: @dubekid